Dedalus Africa
General Editor: Jethro Soutar

The Desert and the Drum

Mbarek Ould Beyrouk

THE DESERT AND THE DRUM

translated by Rachael McGill

Dedalus

This book has been selected to receive financial assistance from English PEN's "PEN translates" programme, supported by Arts Council England. English PEN exists to promote literature and our understanding of it, to uphold writers' freedoms around the world, to campaign against the persecution and imprisonment of writers for stating their views, and to promote the friendly co-operation of writers and the exchange of ideas.

Published in the UK by Dedalus Limited
24-26, St Judith's Lane, Sawtry, Cambs, PE28 5XE
email: info@dedalusbooks.com
www.dedalusbooks.com

ISBN printed book 978 1 910213 79 7
ISBN ebook 978 1 912868 08 7

Dedalus is distributed in the USA & Canada by SCB Distributors
15608 South New Century Drive, Gardena, CA 90248
email: info@scbdistributors.com   web: www.scbdistributors.com

Dedalus is distributed in Australia by Peribo Pty Ltd
58, Beaumont Road, Mount Kuring-gai, N.S.W. 2080
email: info@peribo.com.au

First published by Dedalus in 2018
Le tambour des larmes © Editions Elyzad 2015
Translation copyright © Rachael McGill 2018

The right of Mbarek Ould Beyrouk to be identified as the author and Rachael McGill as the translator of this work has been asserted by them in accordance with the Copyright, Designs and Patents Act, 1988.

Printed and bound in Great Britain by Clays Ltd, Elcograf S.p.A.
Typeset by Marie Lane

The Author

Mbarek Ould Beyrouk (Beyrouk) was born in Atar, Mauritania, in 1957.

A journalist, he founded the country's first ever independent newspaper, *Mauritanie Demain*, in 1988, and is a recognised champion of free speech. In 2006 he was appointed to the Higher Authority for the Printed and Audiovisual Press in Mauritania, and he is currently an advisor to the President of the Republic.

He has written four books, including three novels: *Et le ciel a oublié de pleuvoir* (2006), *Le Griot de l'émir* (2013) and *Le tambour des larmes* (2015).

The Translator

Rachael McGill is a playwright, fiction writer and translator from French, German, Spanish and Portuguese. Her play *The Lemon Princess* is published by Oberon. She has translated many plays, including *Marieluise* (winner of the Gate Theatre Translation Award) and *The Time of the Tortoise*, both by Kerstin Specht, published by Oberon.

There was no moon, no stars. The light had been drained away, the sky left mute. I could distinguish neither colours nor shapes. Dunes and trees had been engulfed by the universe, sucked into its sidereal blackness. I scanned the shadows to left and right, chanting suras to ward off djinns.

I welcomed the obscurity; a gift from nature. It would make it harder for them to find me. The darkness would blind their eyes, the sand storms would scramble their senses and erase my trail. To escape them, all I had to do was keep walking. Not panic, or scream, or cry, just walk. The place I was aiming for was straight ahead, all the herdsmen had said so.

I longed to stop and catch my breath, to release my burden and stretch my arms, loosen my neck, massage out the aches in my body, push the night shadows aside, inhale the air and listen to the quiet sky. Instead I quickened my pace. I told myself I must never weaken, or fall, or forget myself, or forget what was burning inside me: the pain, the anger, the love. I repeated softly that I was myself, not someone else, that I wasn't dreaming, that it was true: I'd cut the ties that bound me to my clan, I'd stolen the object of my tribe's vanity, the keeper of its myths, I'd set out in search of the dreams that kept me awake at night. I had to escape this place forever, whatever it took, keep on moving until I reached the lights in the distance, and, eventually my lost love, my greatest joy, the thing they should never have taken from me.

I had no idea what the future held, who I might meet, what paths I might take; no inkling of the places I might go, where I might live, what awaited me there. I had nothing. No, that wasn't true. It was improbable, perhaps impossible, but I couldn't help feeling a glimmer of hope whenever I thought about Mbarka. I tried not to think too much. Why call out to a silent echo, a tomorrow that can never reply? Why reach for helping hands when you don't know who they belong to? Why ask endless what-ifs, conjure up possibilities that only bring confusion? According to the entire tribe, I was crazy. Why try to think if you're no longer in possession of your senses? All I had was the memory of a flesh that was once my flesh, a blood that was once my blood. Everything else was new terrain I had to conquer, tools I had to master, to get back what was mine.

I was fragile and small, but I was fearless. I was prepared to face the demons of the night and the snakes in the sand, to dive, alone and head first, into the hubbub of the cities. I refused to be intimidated by the chapters of the past or the indecipherable pages of the future. No danger would deter me. I would search for a century if that's what it took. I would fight for a thousand years, scream the name of the soul that I'd lost for another thousand, across all the Saharas of all time.

I felt a flush of pleasure when I imagined the commotion at the camp. My mother's stone-faced death mask would have dropped. She'd be flailing her arms, covering her head with sand. Memed might be crying, in that quiet way he was so good at. My friends would be staring at each other, open-mouthed, speechless for once. The women would be touching the ground with their fingers to ward off evil. The slaves would be laughing under their breath, whispering, 'She's run away from home!' I could see it all: the clouds disappearing abruptly from the sky, the people's incredulity, their confusion, the earth shifting beneath their feet, the hands on hearts, on heads, the fury consuming their bodies, the eyes rolling upwards, the veins pulsing in their temples, and the cries of horror escaping from the strong, hairy chests of the men when they finally realised what had happened, and roared, 'She's taken the drum!'

A dark mass loomed in front of me. I stepped back, rubbed my eyes, then moved forward again with caution, my senses heightened. I'd come upon a herd of camels. They seemed well-fed and peaceful, letting just an occasional soft grunt float up to the sky. Their beige pelts merged with the sand, but the glimmer from their bulbous eyes shone through the thick night. I spotted the herdsman's fire a little distance away. I was aware of my hunger, my exhaustion. How long had I been walking? I no longer had a clear grasp on anything, but I could feel my stomach rumbling, my lungs gasping, drowsiness beginning to invade my limbs and my eyes.

The herdsman was singing, all alone, into the night. His melodious voice filled the air with freshness. I couldn't make out his features, just a thin silhouette. He sang an ancient song intended to repel demons and calm fears. I was tempted to approach him, but I hung back. I couldn't ask to share his food or the heat of his fire. He'd be shocked to see a ragged, distressed woman appearing in the middle of the night; he'd think me a djinn and run from me. The next day he'd tell the other herdsmen he met, and they'd all know which direction I'd taken.

I was wary of walking round the camel herd, in case I got lost: I had to go straight ahead. I was drained. My head spun. My arms had gone to sleep. I stopped and laid my burden down. As I did so, an image flashed before me again, clear as day, of the uproar I'd unleashed at the camp. I saw flames devouring souls, howls bursting from throats, tears, moans and curses hurled in my direction. I saw the chief gazing all around, pained, his eyes filled with death and ancient conquests. I saw him mourning the wound to his blind, ignorant pride. I saw marabouts tracing words in the sand, spells to deprive me of my sight and make me return home. I saw warriors seizing their weapons, vowing to bring me back, dead or alive.

The tribal drum, the *rezzam*, was never allowed to touch the earth, or be held by an impure hand. It was not allowed to leave the heart of the camp. The drum *was* the tribe; its presence, its confidence, its voice. It was our sacred pennant, the flag carried by our fathers and our fathers' fathers. I, Rayhana, had committed an unpardonable sin. I'd choked the tribe's voice, brought shame upon it, castrated the source of its power, razed its tents, insulted its ancestors, and my own. I'd captured the *rezzam*, the sacred *tombol*[1], sullied it with my woman's hands, clasped it to my impure breast. Then I'd let it drop to the ground, touch the earth. It would no longer cast its blessing over the tribe, no longer beat out its warnings of danger, no longer summon brave fighters to their deaths. I'd silenced the drum.

I felt no remorse. I exulted to think of the anger and grief I'd caused. Now they could have their own taste of bitterness and shame; just a tiny portion of pain, nothing compared to

1 Author's note: *Rezzam* and *tombol* are names given to the tribal drum.

the chasm of suffering they'd opened up in me. I'd stolen their drum, but they'd taken my whole being. They'd put me to sleep, then scooped out my guts, my womb, and the little soul that had lived inside it.

I got up again and began to creep forwards, reaching out to stroke the humps of the camels as I passed. They remained kneeling, chewing sleepily at the weeds. Their necks were branded with the symbol of our camp. Which member of the tribe did they belong to? What did I care? I'd severed my connection with the people who'd prevented me from loving. I'd wiped the self-satisfied smiles off their faces. I sat down again, leaned my back against the belly of the plumpest camel and closed my eyes. The aching in my bones gradually subsided, and a little warmth returned to my body. My hunger returned too. I found a battered, foul-smelling tin that someone had discarded. I rinsed it with sand and leaned over to lift the coarse material that covered my camel's udder. I gently milked the beast. Its low grunts came in time with my movements. The sound aroused an ancient connection in me, to things that had been part of me since birth. I drank thirstily, then threw the tin aside. It was time to detach myself from the old ways: I was no longer from here. I was from nowhere, and I was going faraway. Straight ahead.

The night was black. The dunes I had to climb were huge. I stumbled often. I pushed on, panting under the weight of the sacred drum, my feet sinking into the sand. Sometimes I sprawled on my stomach, slid backwards down a slope, then got up and climbed again. I cried and cursed the tribes, the wind, the sand. Arriving at the summit of a dune, I let the drum go. It thudded softly as it rolled down the other side of the sandy slope. I followed it, surrendering to a dizzy fall that propelled me down. I got up, took up my burden again, and resumed my back-breaking walk.

Suddenly my bare toes registered the decisive solidity of a *reg*.[2] I nearly cried out with joy. I'd reached the land of stones, a surface which would graze my feet but would not preserve their imprints: it would be harder for them to track me now. Perhaps I'd already won. I was forced to slow my pace, though, for fear of stumbling against a sharp stone in the dark. My feet became cut and bruised, my legs trembled, my back bowed under the weight of the drum, but I knew I shouldn't stop while I was on the *reg*. I closed my eyes. Through pure force of will, I dragged my faltering body over the harsh terrain.

I don't know how long I walked. The sky still told me nothing. There was no sign of life in any direction. My mind was blank, as if the emptiness all around had seeped inside me. I neither thought nor felt. I was a wandering soul, without agency, existing somewhere beyond fatigue or despair. All I had was a vague sense of the increasing wind, the tempest of sand that came in its wake, the stones lifted by the gusts that hit me in the face and legs, my twisted veil, which sometimes flew out behind me, sometimes wrapped itself around my neck and strangled me. I gripped my burden and moved forwards, falling down, getting up again. I kept walking, because the *reg* is merciless; if you fall, it doesn't help you back to your feet. A single word welled up from deep inside me: 'walk'. When a small hut appeared like an apparition, I collapsed in front of it.

---

2 Translator's note: a *reg*, or desert pavement, is a surface covered with interlocking pebble and cobble-sized rocks.

When I opened my eyes, I was lying on a mat, a pillow beneath my head, the scent of rancid butter in my nostrils. Above me loomed the large, calm, copper-coloured face of a woman. Her forehead was creased with small wrinkles. Wisps of her white hair poked out from under a black veil that smelled of dust and sweat.

She showed a white-toothed smile that dispelled my fears: I wasn't dead, I hadn't fallen into their hands. I looked around me. The first rays of sunlight were filtering through the straw roof of the hut, the dark interior beginning to bow to the authority of the day. There was very little furniture: two mattresses on the ground, a scrap of old carpet, a frayed, narrow mat, some faded cushions piled up in the corner, a broken suitcase, another hooked on a wooden pole, a man's clothes hanging from a beam.

The woman gave me some very sweet corn porridge. I felt my strength returning.

'May God repay you a hundred times for your kind deeds,' I told her weakly.

'Rest, my dear. You're exhausted.'

'Where am I?'

'You're in Hamdoun, my dear.'

'Hamdoun?!'

Tears came to my eyes. I'd walked so far. I never would've thought it possible to cover so much ground in one night.

'Don't cry, my child,' the woman said. 'It's over now. You're safe. I saw you collapsing, just as the sun rose.'

'I thought I was dying,' I murmured.

'I thought you were an apparition sent by a djinn!' She had

13

a smile as sweet as a rainy season morning.

'I must have looked like a djinn,' I said.

'Your cheeks were all streaked with tears. Djinns don't cry.'

'I walked for a long time. I was carrying the weight of the world.'

'Yes. A tam tam.'

'A drum. Our drum!' Despite my weakness, I instinctively raised my voice. I glanced around me.

'It's just there, my child,' the woman said. She pointed at the *rezzam*, thrown into a corner of the hut. It was on a mat, between a grubby cushion and a crude water jug. It did not look out of place in that humble setting. It did not shine in the midst of the rags around it. In spite of myself, I was amazed. The sacred drum of the great tribe sat, placid and sheepish, in a peasant's hut. It did not cry. It did not protest.

'You're carrying an old drum with you?' the woman asked me.

'Yes,' I said, 'it's an old drum, but it's worth all the drums on earth.'

'I understand,' she said. 'Some things don't have a price.'

I was suddenly afraid of giving myself away. I summoned all my strength and stood up. 'I must leave,' I said. A shiver ran through my body. Flashes of light exploded like fireworks inside my head.

'No, no, you must rest,' the woman said. She took me by the shoulders. 'You're not well. I can't let you leave now. You can go later. The sand storm is over, but now it looks like rain. You must've had a very hard night.'

'I wandered off the path and lost my caravan,' I lied.

14

Remembering the drum, I added 'I'm a griotte[3].'

The woman didn't seem especially impressed.

'I guessed as much when I saw the drum. Which family are you from?'

I gave a name, one I'd heard somewhere.

'I don't know that name, but no griot has ever come to this oasis. I'm glad you ended up here. You can stay and rest for as long as you need to.'

I wanted to shower the woman with thanks again, to kiss her hands and feet, to pray out loud for her life to be long, but tiredness invaded my whole being. My eyes no longer obeyed me; I sank into a deep sleep.

I had a disturbing dream. I was at the bottom of a well, holding a baby in my arms. I was crying to the world, 'Let us live! At least let him live!' No one was listening. My only witnesses were a cold patch of unforgiving sky and the smooth walls of the well that threatened to cave in on us. The water had reached my stomach and was still rising. The baby was crying. I hugged him and shouted over and over for help, but no one came.

I woke with a start. Daylight now fully occupied the house. A light smoke floated on the air. The woman had her hand on my forehead and was murmuring an incantation. A thick, dirty *burnous*[4] had been draped over me. A man stood with his back to me, stirring something on a small stove.

'You were shouting, my child,' said the woman. 'You were terrified. Repeat after me: *bismillah rahman rahim*.'

---

3 Translator's note: griotte is the feminine form of griot, a West African wandering poet and musician who passes on oral storytelling traditions.
4 Translator's note: a long, hooded Arab cloak.

I repeated the sacred words for expelling demons. I tried to throw the *burnous* aside, but the woman stopped me with a quick gesture, her eyes flicking towards the man, still absorbed in his task. I realised that underneath the *burnous* I was practically naked. The bottom of my veil had torn off, and my dress exposed my stomach and breasts. I curled myself into a ball.

The man turned round and put a plate down on the mat. He began to throw scraps of meat on to it as he removed them from the fire. He did not cast a single glance in my direction. He was around forty, with an earthy complexion, a small white beard and the beginnings of a bald patch on his head. He wore a faded blue *boubou*[5]. His torso showed through a torn shirt. He had a mark on his forehead and a sneer on his lips. I disliked him immediately. I've always felt that men who don't look at women are hiding something, that their indifference is a disguise for something unpleasant. But despite my misgivings, we enjoyed an excellent *méchoui*[6]. Afterwards, the man served us tea. I felt stronger again, and allowed myself to feel a little hope. The omens were good. I'd survived the white sands, the *reg* and the wind, and, on the outskirts of the city, I'd found a kind heart. My whole body ached, but I wasn't dead. Soon I could be on my way again, to search for my little lost soul.

'May God shower his blessings on you,' I said. 'May he fill your cupboards and your hearts, may he remove hunger and thirst from your lives.'

'We did no more than our duty – welcoming a guest.'

'You saved my life, and you gave me the smile of generous

5 Translator's note: a long, flowing robe.
6 Translator's note: spit-roasted lamb.

16

souls. I don't even know who you are.'

'My name is Rahma,' said the woman. 'My husband and I are from the Chella tribe. It's an offshoot of the Ghassem.'

'*Wakhyertt!*[7] That's good blood! I'm...'

I stopped myself. I'd been about to reveal my true affiliation. I was still afraid the tribe would pursue me.

I invented a new first name and repeated the surname I'd already given. It felt shameful to lie to someone so kind. My heart clenched with remorse, but I had no choice.

Rahma noticed my hesitation. The man did too. He lifted his eyes to me for the first time.

'*Wakhyertt,*' he said hesitantly.

'I must leave,' I said. 'I must go to the city and look for my people.'

'Won't you stay a little longer?'

'May God repay you a thousand times over for the kindness you've offered me. But I can't stay. The others will be waiting.'

The woman got up. 'Very well,' she said, 'but you'll go on the back of a donkey this time. Mahmoud will take you to town. The road is long, and you're still tired.'

She left the room. Her husband followed, in response to some imperceptible sign. She returned holding a long dress, drab but clean, a thick veil and a pair of old sandals.

'I know you young people wear lighter, more colourful clothes now, but at least with this you can go into the city without shame.'

I thanked her again profusely, evoking the names of all the saints I knew.

---

7 Author's note: Exclamation meaning something like 'a good family.'

The sun's fury had abated by the time we took to the road. Clouds travelled with us, sometimes covering us with their flighty shadows.

'Those are rain clouds.' said Mahmoud. 'We must get there before evening.'

We climbed a mountainside. I was amazed to see a green oasis unfolding below us. I'd noticed nothing when I arrived, blinded by the night, my tiredness, my distress. This vast expanse of green had been spread beneath my feet all the time, concealed between the dunes and the rock.

Palms snaked in a gracious blue arc along the length of the *wadi*[8]. The wind produced soft musical sounds as it caressed them. At the bottom, mountain and sand met, holding their little universe in a protective embrace. A glint up ahead suggested there was even a waterhole.

'You have a very beautiful oasis,' I said to Mahmoud.

'Yes. If the rains come this year, the *guetna*, our date harvest, will be good. The palms haven't got sick yet.'

'The palm trees get sick?'

'Yes, they get all sorts of illnesses and afflictions. A palm tree is just like a man.'

'Do you have palm trees of your own?'

'We used to, a long time ago. They were destroyed by drought and by an awful sickness called the *bayoud*. Now we just work for the owners who live in the cities. They only come here in summer.'

'It must be good to live in an oasis, surrounded by all this green. Do a lot of people live here?'

'Very few people live here outside the summer and the date

---

8 Translator's note: Arabic term for a valley.

harvest. There are no other businesses, as you can see. We have to go to the city for supplies. Our boss sometimes forgets to pay us for several months. And the work can be very hard.'

The donkey panted as it climbed the stony slope. Mahmoud led it by a short rope. He fell silent, concentrating on negotiating the narrow path. My thoughts returned to my camp, the scandal of my departure. How had Memed reacted? Had he taken my side? How could I expect him to understand when I'd abandoned him without a word? Would he be miserable, appear in public with his head bowed? My mother, I knew, would've cried at first, not for me but because of the shame I'd caused her, then she would've torn at her hair, then lapsed into an indignant silence, uttering not one word. She would be looking at people absently, as if she didn't understand what they were saying. Her only fear would be that our secret might be revealed, our dishonour, as she called it when we were alone. Family honour meant more to her than her daughter's happiness.

What did I care for tribe or honour? I'd cut the ties that bound me to the camp, left hesitation and remorse behind. I'd begun my quest to find the part of me they'd taken away, to reunite him with my loving arms.

We continued along the steep, rough path. Mahmoud chanted ancient poems in a low voice. The clouds gathered above us. It was as if they'd arranged a meeting to discuss bestowing their generosity upon the earth, I thought, then had to remind myself I'd left the old life behind. I should no longer be fantasising about clouds and greenery: rain from now on would not bring happiness but trouble, anxiety and memories. Still I couldn't help recalling wonderful rainy seasons of the past: tents abandoned, shouts flying up to the sky, fear and hope written on faces, my mother singing old laments, nostalgic and happy, beneath our big, drooping tent.

Mahmoud took larger steps now, spurred on by the threat of rain. He glanced at the sky and muttered prayers.

'The rain's about to come,' he told me. 'A good rain, I think. We need to find shelter.'

I could see no shelter anywhere. Mahmoud led us off the path, towards the side of the mountain.

I was worried. 'Won't we get lost if we go off the path?' I asked.

'No,' he said, 'the city is close, we're up above it now and all roads lead down into it. It's not far, but I know a cave that will shelter us if the rain comes.'

We heard loud rumbles. The sky turned red, the wind began to whistle. Mahmoud led the donkey and me towards the mountainside. I put my hands over my eyes, tried to tame the monsters threatening to rear up inside me. I hadn't trembled in the dark night, the gaping jaws of the desert, the black wind of the *reg*. This was just a bit of rain, the last before I reached the edge of the unknown. It was not the drum taking its vengeance. The drum was nothing but some wood and a scrap of cow skin.

A gap in the rocks opened its arms to us and we entered the belly of the mountain. It was dark and cold. Mahmoud took a torch from the large pocket of his *boubou* and shone light into the cave. It was high and deep, as if made to protect and receive. I gave a loud shout to frighten off any beasts that might be lurking at the back, or to wake up the spirits sleeping there. The echo returned my voice to me. Mahmoud switched off the torch. I took it from him and turned it on again, pointing it into the cave as I moved forward. I was trembling with fear, but curious too. Mahmoud remained at the entrance, watching the rain.

I noticed odd markings traced in red pigment on the walls: drawings of strange animals, long-limbed beings, indecipherable arabesques. I was about to call to Mahmoud, but he seemed engrossed by the rain. He prayed loudly as he watched it fall. His voice was tuneless, like a stone hurtling down a mountainside. I caressed the coloured rock with my hands. I remembered what Memed had told me about men from long ago who wore animal skins and drew images on walls. They didn't speak the language of humans and didn't know God or his prophets. I was fascinated by the traces left by these ancient hands, long-gone, but their signs still there for me, greetings from the depths of time. They told me people had been here: a young woman like me, perhaps, lost like me, perhaps, who had loved and suffered like me. These monsters were what she saw and what she feared; that squiggle I didn't know how to read was her joy, or her anxiety, or her fear, or even her name, yes, perhaps she'd written her name, or the name of her lover. It was inscribed there for eternity, in a language long dead.

The rain eased a little. I listened with pleasure to its pattering harmonies. I'd turned off the torch so as not to drain its fading batteries. My eyes had become accustomed to the dark. I gradually forgot the presence of Mahmoud, my dislocation, even the ancient cave artists I'd been communing with across time. I saw, dream-like, the figure of a child running naked over a white dune, with me chasing behind him, laughing. Then suddenly it was Mahmoud I saw. He was coming towards me, feeling his way in the dark. I stood still, stunned. His body collided with mine, his hands groped towards my breasts. I stepped back, thinking he must've got confused in the gloom; but he pushed himself up against me, a dark shadow contorting his face, a horrible leer forming on his mouth. I tried to shove him away, crying, 'You've gone crazy, Mahmoud! I'm your guest, Rahma's guest!'

He put his arms around me and tried to kiss me. I felt his hardness against me, his fetid mouth bite at my cheek. He breathed heavily, uttered incomprehensible words. I braced myself against the cave wall, then, in a sudden movement, I squirmed away from him and hit him in the face. He let go of me. I hurled myself towards the entrance of the cave. He came after me and caught me straightaway, pushed me down on to my back, collapsed with his full weight on top of me, still breathing heavily. I fumbled around with a trembling hand, grabbed a stone and struck it against him with all my strength. He cried out. His hands flew to his face. I felt his blood spilling on to my throat and breasts. I pushed him away as hard as I could and staggered outside. The drum was lying by the entrance to the cave. I grabbed it with both hands and ran. The rain continued to hammer down and the shadows of night had covered the earth again. I could see lights glimmering in the distance. It could only be the city. All routes led to it, the wicked Mahmoud had said.

Monsters of iron and steel appeared one day from nowhere. No one had warned us they were coming. First we heard an enormous roar. Some people thought it was thunder, but the sky remained an unblemished blue. Others turned their eyes towards the mountains; the faraway summits stood steadfast and serene. The earth began to tremble beneath our feet. We listened, worried, and strained our eyes towards the horizon. In the distance, a cloud of ochre dust rose towards the sky. We remained immobile, gaping at this sight for which we had no name. When we realised the rumbling and the storm were coming towards us, panic spread like wildfire: people ran to hide behind dunes or collect livestock, men went to get their guns, women grabbed their children and ran inside tents. The tribal drum sounded to summon those who were away from the camp. We watched, stunned and powerless, as the terrible unknown thing approached.

Then it stopped. The dust swelled and began to dissipate, until we could make out terrible giants emerging from it: a machine the like of which even those who had been to the city had never seen, huge lorries with colossal structures mounted on top of them. There were people too, swarming around the machines. We glanced at each other, understanding nothing. What were these people and their monsters of steel doing just a mile from our camp? Men jumped from the lorries and pulled down huge trunks and long planks. They began to erect small, misshapen tents made from crude cloths. These tents had neither poles nor decoration and went up in the blink of an eye. The men also built tiny houses of wood, unrolled cables, panted as they pushed trollies loaded with large iron boxes, which they lowered to the ground with care.

We assembled on the big dune overlooking our camp to observe them. They had no livestock, no women, no children. Some were black, some white. Some were bare-chested. They moved constantly, like ants. They weren't a tribe, nor were they soldiers. We had no idea what they were. We looked to each other for answers, but no one had an explanation. The whispers began: they'd come to take our land, our wells would dry up, they would burn the vegetation when the rains came.

Our men conferred all night in the chief's tent and came to no conclusion. The next day, after a morning of confusion and hesitation, the chief announced he would go down, alone, to meet the new arrivals. He was gone for a long time. We waited on tenterhooks. When he finally returned, the drum sounded, calling the whole tribe to meet outside his tent. Even the girls were authorised to attend.

The chief seemed concerned. He began by trying to reassure us. Loud sounds of metal grating on metal sometimes drowned out his voice, but we understood that he was saying we should not be alarmed, that the people down there were not an enemy tribe, or looters, that they would not stay forever, and that they had the permission of the government. They would stay for a few months, then leave. They didn't need the water from our wells or the vegetation from our pastures, they could even help us sometimes if we needed them to, for example to treat us if we were sick. Most of them were not from our country. Their bosses were *Nçaras*, completely white people from Europe, who had our languages translated for them but could listen and understand well enough. They were going to sniff the earth, or something like that, as far as he had understood, to try to find metals, or gold or oil perhaps, but they weren't doing that work here, they were sending teams to other places, faraway, to open up the earth and dig down into it. They were just using this spot to rest and sleep. The chief said none of us should approach the strangers' camp. We could still take our livestock wherever we wanted, we could continue our daily lives just as before, but we shouldn't go near their area. He would go and speak to their chief from time to time, if necessary, but no one else should go there. That way peace would continue to reign between us and no one would have any cause for complaint. The strangers, he said in conclusion, seemed to be powerful, a thousand times richer and more powerful than our humble tribe, or any of the tribes we knew. They had the government behind them, and we didn't want to get into difficulties with *Nçaras* or with the government. He stopped speaking and lifted his hand in a weary gesture. His sunken eyes searched the room. I knew my uncle: he was anticipating questions to which he had no answers.

But nobody asked any questions. We didn't understand much either, but we looked around at each other and nodded our heads. No one spoke because no one could think of the words. All the same, we were disturbed. We felt the vague sensation that strange things had crept into our world, that they would cause disruption of a lasting nature, of a nature we didn't know how to name because it didn't exist in our language, rich as it was. The older people fingered their long strings of prayer beads and mouthed resigned *inch'Allah*s. The young people expressed their restlessness without words.

It was as if several rungs had broken off the ladder of our routines. The days began to be dictated by elements outside our control. In the mornings, we were woken by alien noises. The cries of our muezzin, the calls of our herdsmen, the grunts of our camels, the bleating of our sheep, had all become weak and inaudible. The voices and the motors of the strangers filled up all the space. Our evenings were taken from us too, because that was when they came back to their camp: their car engines continued to roar into the night, and we heard them singing, shouting and laughing. Their powerful lights sometimes illuminated the tops of our tents. From the moment they arrived, the strangers stole something essential from us, without us feeling we had the right to protest.

A malaise invaded our spirits. Anger began to brew inside the tents. A number of people expressed the opinion that we should move our camp elsewhere. The chief opposed the idea. He thought it would be wrong to abandon our land just because others had arrived on it. 'We're no longer really nomadic people,' he said. 'We've learned to stay in one place, and this is the place we've chosen. Why should we desert it? Let's try to rise above these irritations – they will pass!' Eventually everyone agreed that my uncle was right.

Without discussing it further, we all worked hard to ignore the new arrivals. We stopped climbing the highest dune to look down at them, we no longer talked about them, we pretended we couldn't hear when their lorries filled the air with noise first thing in the morning and at sunset. We terrified our youngest members out of approaching them by saying they ate children. Even our animals no longer strayed in the direction of their camp. We closed our eyes to them because, deep down, we were ashamed we had allowed their presence to be imposed on us, ashamed of our failure to understand it, to confidently accept or reject it.

In keeping with tradition, however, the chief ordered that we sacrifice a camel, prepare a sumptuous feast and go and offer it to the *Nçaras*. He explained we were only doing it because it was our tradition, that it didn't represent a gesture of friendship towards the nameless strangers. They would accept the offering, and that would be the end of the exchange. We'd quickly realised they were avoiding us too. They never approached our well or our camp. Their lorries never drove too close to our tents. Their men never came among us, and if they passed us, they didn't pause or make even the tiniest hand gesture in our direction. We too looked away, pretended to be distracted by something. We lived in two separate universes. That seemed to suit everyone.

The only person who remained completely indifferent to the appearance of the foreigners was my mother. But very little affected my mother; she was unmoved by bad winds, harsh winters or droughts. She had crossed the Sahara of doubt long ago, never to return. She watched, expressionless, as life passed her by. She didn't frown, didn't question, didn't fret. The only thing that troubled her was seeing her brother troubled. As soon as she saw anxiety written on his face, she'd fly into a panic, as if the earth were about to swallow us up, searching frantically for the source of his anger.

She'd organised her life around her older brother, and him alone, ever since she was a child. She sought his approval before making even the most insignificant decision. She loved only what he loved, rejected whatever he didn't like.

My father had loathed his wife's obsession. He forbade her from seeking the chief's approval in everything, and from mentioning Sheik Ahmed all the time. My mother ignored his complaints. She couldn't help it; she was chained. My father continued to object. His antipathy towards my uncle grew by the day, until he ended up hating him. One morning, sick of the constant spectre of Sheik Ahmed in his life, my father left the camp and my mother, setting out with nothing but a small bundle on his back. He shouted, loud enough for everyone to hear, that he was leaving forever, turning his back on life in a tent ruled by an authority other than his own, in a camp controlled by an incompetent chief. He would no longer bow to Sheik Ahmed's will, and he would go somewhere he would never hear that name spoken. From that moment onwards he disowned family, clan and tribe.

I was six years old when my father left. I have only a vague memory of a tall figure with bushy hair, a clearer one of the sensation of his thick beard prickling my cheeks when he kissed me. I always listened carefully when people talked about him, not realising I was there or thinking me too young to understand. They described an angry, brutal man, whose hatred for his cousin, the chief, was out of all proportion, a man whose bad character and rebellious spirit had pushed him towards a life bereft of family, livestock, tent or tribe. I was the daughter of a renegade.

When my father left, my mother ceased to care about her appearance. The woman who had turned so many heads in her youth stopped grooming herself, no longer put kohl on her eyes or rubbed butter into her body, no longer burned incense in our tent. She wore a thick veil and a gloomy expression.

Still, we weren't poor. My father had left behind everything he possessed, and he was one of the richest men in the camp. Our tent was more than twenty spans wide, even more spacious and beautiful than that of the chief. It was made of black wool, with sturdy flaps. It had taken all the women of the camp a month to sew it. The best of our artists had decorated it with fantastic arabesques; we had numerous, colourful cushions; our floor was covered with thick, silky animal hides; our utensils made by the best blacksmiths. The tent kept out both rain and wind; the women of the camp liked to say that it breathed the weather.

We had lots of plump, white camels, as well as goats and ewes. We had servants to look after them. But my mother handed the task of managing this fortune over to her brother. She wanted nothing for herself. She said she had no ambitions other than to please God and see her daughter grow up and make a good marriage. If she missed my father, she never said so. The only help she accepted to run our small household was that of Mbarka. People pitied my mother and praised her faith and humility, yet her pride in her ancestry never left her; she claimed to be descended from the noblest Saharan families. She evoked her ancestors morning and night, prayed for the souls of the many amongst them who had spent their lives raiding and stealing, as well as those who had lived in faith.

She cherished them all, the bandits and the imams. The former were heroes in her eyes, the latter saints.

Gradually, life at the camp returned to its normal pattern. The men took the camels out to graze all day, the old people gossiped in their tents, the boys studied the sacred texts and fetched water from the wells, the women looked after the homes and the domestic animals, the blacksmiths worked at their fires, the slaves and the freed slaves helped with the odd jobs around the camp. My friends and I, the girls from good families, concentrated on fattening ourselves up so we would be beautiful and get good husbands, and most of all on telling stories in which dashing princes fell in love with pretty young Bedouins.

We girls were in the habit of meeting in the evenings on top of a dune to sing, dance and talk. We played the old tunes we knew, using a jerry can as a drum. The boys of the camp came along too. They listened to our singing and complimented us, trying to impress us by appearing intelligent and spiritual. Sometimes one of them would compose a *gav*, a little quatrain, in praise of the beauty of one of us. We laughed and applauded. At other times the boys competed in poetic jousts for our favour. We were charmed and encouraged their playful rivalry. Tentative flirtations began, beneath the watchful gaze of the matrons who sat at a little distance, keeping an eye on us while pretending to be asleep.

One evening a young man appeared, a stranger. We hadn't seen him approach. He wore a black turban, a blue *boubou* and a white shirt, all spotlessly clean. A watch glinted on his wrist. He held a strange machine in his hand. He greeted us. One

of the boys returned the greeting, then we all fell silent. The
girls didn't even dare look at him. We were intimidated by his
clothes, the cigarette in his mouth, the thing in his hand, which
made crackling noises, and to which he sometimes spoke, a
single foreign word that meant nothing to us. We glanced at
each other, uncertain, then began to get up. The boys prepared
to confront him. He ignored them and spoke to us:

'Where are you going, sisters? I'm not a djinn. I'm just a
brother who's come to say hello and compliment you on your
lovely singing.'

His tone wasn't rude, just a little mocking.

One of the boys moved towards him, threatening.

'What have you come here for, man?'

'I just told you. To compliment these girls on their beautiful
voices. Perhaps even to compose some verses better than the
ones I've just heard.'

'Where did you come from?' asked another of the boys.

'From down there! I didn't fall from the sky!' He pointed
at the foreigners' camp.

'We don't have anything to do with the people down there.
The understanding is that you stay in your place and we stay
in ours.'

'I never agreed to that "understanding". And down there
is not "my place". I'm a stranger here. Is this the way your
tribe greets strangers? I'm a guest, and all I want is to stay
for a while and listen to these girls. I think you're forgetting
yourselves.'

The boys didn't answer. They looked at each other, taken
off guard by the stranger's rebuke. He was right that all guests
should receive a courteous welcome. The arrival of the camp of

foreigners had disturbed not just our habits, but our emotions as well. There was another awkward silence. Then we, the girls, sat back down and softly resumed our singing. After a moment, one of the boys ran to the nearest tent and came back with a teapot, cups and some wood charcoal. He dug a hole in the sand, started a fire and began to prepare tea for the guest. The boys were eager to uphold our traditions, but they were disturbed by the stranger's presence: something wasn't right. They eyed each other, still undecided. The stranger smoked serenely. When he spoke, his tone was calm, with just the tiniest hint of irritation.

'I didn't mean to invade your privacy, or spoil the atmosphere. I was drawn to your group. I've heard you laughing and singing every night, and I was bored down there, with all those men who don't understand anything about anything. The voices of these girls reminded me of a world I knew as a child, a world I thought I'd lost forever. I hesitated for a long time before coming. I'll go away again if you like.'

Everyone protested. We asked him to stay.

'I'm actually from a tribe related to yours,' he added, 'if you are, as I think you are, the Oulad Mahmoud. I'm from the Oulad Ethmane. My name is Yahya Ould Ahmed Ould Sidi Ould Ethmane.'

The boys immediately surrounded him.

'Why didn't you say so? This is your home! Our tribes have been allies for years. There isn't even a blood debt between us! You should've introduced yourself!'

'Didn't really get a chance,' he said, laughing.

They all burst out laughing too, and started to shake hands. Delighted with this turn of events, we, the girls, forgot our jerry can drum and bombarded the stranger with questions: what was the foreigners' camp? What was the thing in his hand that crackled? What were they really doing down there? Was it true they didn't drink water? Why didn't they have wells? Was it true they were extracting things from the ground? Why didn't they have any women or children?

He laughed and answered our questions simply, with humour. We learned that the device in his hand allowed him to stay in contact with people faraway, that at the camp they had very big basins that could hold enough water to last a long time, that the company he worked for belonged to *Nçaras*, westerners who were looking for gold and precious metals.

We were disappointed to hear he worked for others: only slaves or low-caste people worked for others. How could a young man from a good family accept servitude?

'Don't mind them,' said one of the boys, laughing. 'They're little Bedouins who know nothing of the world.' He turned to us and explained that in the city, people worked for companies, the government, even for other people. There was no dishonour in it.

Then Memed spoke. He said, 'It's true that in the city they know nothing about honour.'

His tone was angry. We all knew that Memed, the only one of us to have been educated elsewhere, hated the city and everything that came from it. But his jibe surprised us: he was normally a person of few words, and they were always polite. We resumed our singing. The stranger turned out to be an elegant speaker. He even knew how to compose a *gav*. To my amazement, he addressed his poem to me. It praised the brightness of my gazelle-like eyes, which he couldn't see in the dark, and the lightness of my steps on the sand, which he had never witnessed. All the same, I was pleased. I stammered some timid words of thanks that made everyone laugh at me.

He returned on other evenings, bringing incredible offerings: sweets, chocolates, butter biscuits, cakes, fruit. Delighted, we stuffed them all into our mouths then and there, knowing we couldn't take offerings from one of the strangers back to the camp. At first the boys sulkily refused the gifts, then they agreed to keep the secret and joined in our feasting. Only Memed stopped coming to our meetings after that.

Yahya became a regular in our circle, a friend to the boys, to whom he was like a generous and knowledgeable older brother, and courteous with the girls, who thought him very respectable. Every evening he composed a small poem in honour of my eyes, my smile, my voice. I was flattered and started to regard him with interest. He was very brown, nearly black, with even features, a full mouth and a high forehead. He wore no turban, and his hair was wild and flowing. He wasn't what you'd call handsome, he didn't fit the image we'd created of the noble prince who would carry us away on a golden litter to a faraway land, but there was something bold in his glance that made him intriguing.

Our mothers weren't sure how to react when they found out Yahya had been spending time with us. It seemed he was from a good family, part of a tribe allied to ours, so perhaps he was trustworthy. Memed argued that no one really knew anything about him, he was arrogant, he worked with foreigners, he hadn't presented himself to the chief, or asked for the hand of one of the girls. But after some deliberation, our mothers relaxed their surveillance. They didn't forbid us from associating with him, but told us to be on our guard.

The other new arrival at the camp, of lesser interest to us girls, was the teacher. Our chief had travelled to the city to ask that a classroom be opened at our camp. The authorities had been putting us off for some time: there was a school in a larger camp not far from ours. Why could we not send our children there? The chief explained that sending our offspring to be educated at a rival camp would be tantamount to conceding the superiority of that camp, which was out of the question for us. If the state wanted our children to be schooled, and wanted to remain neutral in matters of tribal conflict, it should provide a classroom just for us, alongside our tents. He'd helped the education ministry official understand his point of view by taking along two plump camels and two fat ewes.

A large tent had been erected next to the chief's. Long mats had been laid on the floor and a blackboard had been brought from the city. The chief had even placed a spear outside the tent to hold a sign that said in large, proud letters 'CAMP PRIMARY SCHOOL.'

The administration had trouble finding a teacher prepared to go to a school in the middle of the desert. The teachers who were offered the position all used every means at their disposal, including corruption, to wriggle out of it. It was both to punish him and to get rid of him that the authorities finally sent us Ahmed Salem.

He was in his thirties, short and slight, but strong. He had a shaved head, inexpressive eyes, hollow cheeks and a small beard which he tinted with henna and liked to stroke. He dressed in a white *jellaba*[9] and was always mumbling prayers.

9 Translator's note: loose wool or cotton garment with sleeves and a hood.

The chief had furnished the school tent well for him, but when he wasn't teaching, Salem preferred to strut around the camp, hands clasped behind his back, interacting with whoever he met; telling a woman to cover herself more completely, encouraging young people to pray, describing the hell fires of Gehenna to a group of nomads who listened attentively, then got up and immediately forgot everything they'd just heard. He had a radio that he often listened to. He would report to the men about what was going on in the world, quoting important names. People listened in silence and smiled as he moved away. Then they laughed and said 'what do we care what happens in those places? It's another universe. The quarrels and wars of distant people have nothing to do with us.'

The teacher enjoyed expounding on the threats represented by the new camp. The strangers, he said, had come with the help of our corrupt leaders to exploit our resources. They were modern-day Satans leading debauched and impious lives, and we should keep our distance from them. The hate he harboured for the new arrivals was accepted by everyone, but his diatribes against the government displeased the chief. My uncle summoned him and explained that we were only a small camp, part of a medium-sized tribe, and we didn't want to attract the wrath of the state. After that, Ahmed Salem's criticism of the city leaders became more veiled. In return, the chief began to invite him often to his tent. Sheikh Ahmed appreciated the teacher because, unlike the teachers allocated to other camps, he always turned up for work. We were proud that our school was growing. We even began to welcome children from other tribes.

One of Ahmed Salem's diatribes was against the custom we girls had of meeting every evening, with too many boys in attendance, and singing songs with lyrics he considered too light-hearted. He spoke to the chief and the other older men of the camp about it. Some sympathised, others laughed and maliciously suggested he join our group, others told him it was an old tradition and not his concern; most just looked away, bored. When the mothers heard of his complaint, they said they had no intention of bullying their daughters and preventing them from enjoying themselves. They taunted him, 'When you have your own daughter, you can bury her alive if that's what you want!' The matter was dropped.

By this time my friends all considered Yahya to be my rightful match. I protested, but secretly I was flattered. He was my first suitor, unless you counted Memed. According to the other girls, Memed liked me. He'd never indicated this directly, but I had noticed him sneaking glances at me, surreptitiously, as if he was doing wrong. He was a taciturn person who rarely contributed to the conversation. He was turned inwards, his eyes full of sadness, as if he carried the weight of the world on his shoulders. He'd grown up and been educated in a rich family in the city. His paternal uncle was a merchant who still lived in the city and was involved in politics. This man was our camp's main benefactor. Memed could speak French, apparently, and even owned books. He sometimes told us stories about the world. He was polite and obliging. He did have good qualities, but we girls found him boring. We'd formed that opinion the day he returned to the camp, and never changed it.

Yahya was 'the other', the visitor from afar who knew so

many things. All the girls in the camp had tried to charm him, but it was me he'd chosen. I knew my friends envied me the attention from someone so exotic. It didn't take long for me to fall for his spontaneous declarations: he told me he loved me more than anything in the world, that he would prefer any word from me, even an insult, to owning all the kingdoms of the north and entry to paradise in the hereafter. I was innocent and foolish, intoxicated by the promise of forbidden passion. I allowed him to get close to me.

The gestures of affection between us were tentative at first; tiny pebbles of love cast across the space between us: a brief wink, a swift, audacious brush of the hand. We were never alone together; it would have been unimaginable for a young couple to separate themselves from the group, that would be shameful, and our friends would never have allowed it. We contented ourselves with talking to each other whenever the others were busy with their own conversations or songs. I didn't know what to say to him, but he told me fantastic stories of the distant lands that he said he would take me to: roads as wide as all of our *wadis*, with real cars travelling on them, not the crude trucks we saw coming from the strangers' camp, but small, beautiful cars; lights that never ended and buildings that reached the sky. He told me we would travel on planes, like the ones I saw passing in the distance, way above our heads, leaving white trails behind them like clouds. Every evening, as I watched their lights blinking across the sky, I tried to picture myself sitting in one. It was impossible: it made me feel dizzy.

When my friends urged Yahya to ask for my hand, he laughed and said, 'What's the hurry?'

Everything acquired a new intensity. Whenever Yahya's fingertips brushed mine, whenever he stole the lightest caress, right in the middle of speaking to the others, I felt it like a current passing between us, a sweet yet terrifying sting.

One night when I was sleeping deeply, a hand pinched my nose. I woke, dumbfounded and trembling. The hand moved to my mouth. A voice whispered in my ear, 'It's me, Yahya, it's me!' My mother was snoring on the other side of the tent, just a few metres away. I was shaking. Yahya told me in a low voice that he loved me. His hands travelled all over my body. He kissed me. I was afraid. I told myself I must be dreaming. I opened my eyes as wide as I could, but he was still there. I was half-undressed and he was there with me, in the dark. I couldn't imagine the scandal if my mother woke, if someone saw us, if my uncle found out. I would die, surely, and Yahya would too. He continued to press himself against me. I couldn't speak for fear of waking my mother. I fought against the desire that rose up in me and I was so afraid.

The next evening, when we met with the others, I couldn't say a word. I was still stunned by the intrusion of Yahya into our tent. He behaved just as he had on every other evening, laughing as if nothing had happened, reciting old poems, whispering sweet nothings in my ear. I stared at him and began to doubt. Perhaps it had all been a dream, the work of my imagination.

He came again on other nights. I was scared, but there was nothing I could do. I knew I would be the first to be blamed, and I didn't know what would happen to me. Yahya was oblivious to the danger; he would just slip between the sleeping tents and then appear at my bedside. I was staggered by his recklessness.

If my mother had woken, she would have screamed to the heavens, and he and I would've been be flayed on the spot. I didn't know what to do. I sometimes murmured quietly to him that he was crazy, to which he replied, 'Yes, about you.' Sometimes I let tears fall, but it was no good. Despite myself, I began to lie awake waiting for his arrival, anticipating the instant I would see his shadowy figure creeping towards me.

The sky refused to be still. I felt crushed beneath its weight as it flashed and growled around me. Raindrops splattered my face and legs. I staggered under the weight of the drum. It kept trying to escape from me, but I clung on tight. The rain had waited so many months to arrive; why did it have to choose this moment? As soon as I had the thought I regretted it – it was impious to complain about rain, a special blessing from the heavens – but I was soaked to the skin. My head and my garments were heavy. I stumbled through puddles, grazed my knees on rough stones. My clothes were torn yet again and I was exhausted. I could no longer see the lights, but I told myself it was impossible to get lost. That was what the wicked Mahmoud had said.

I avoided the *reg* and the stones and found a soft path. My feet sank into the mud. I removed the sandals and held them in my hands, trying not to slip. I still couldn't make out the glow of the city. Then a flash of lightning illuminated a broad path ahead of me, shrubs trembling in the wind, houses in the distance. I could see no human life, but then I spotted a car, just one, the kind Yahya had described, its lights slicing the air, showing me the way. The driver probably didn't even see me. I passed the first houses. They seemed uninhabited and lifeless. The rain licked at their mud walls and made pattering sounds as it reached the earth. Water splashed loudly from gutters. No voices could be heard behind the high closed doors, the small low windows. Everything was silent and cold. The city of Atar was not exactly welcoming me with open arms; it was ignoring me. It was fast asleep, possibly dead. How could people sleep through rain like this? I tried to shout, but my voice was hoarse. The silence and the emptiness scared me. I remembered what I'd been told of the dangers of the city, a place of perpetual sin and crime, according to my mother. Feeling weak, I began to search for a place to rest. I found a house with a porch in front of it that offered some shelter. I approached on tiptoe and curled up there. Some warmth returned to my limbs, but I couldn't shake off my tiredness. My shoulders felt as if they were about to detach themselves from my body and leave me, my back seemed to be breaking. My legs longed to stretch out, but there wasn't enough space. The drum fell out of my hands. I picked it up again. I felt horribly alone, prey to evil forces. I watched the rain, the only witness to my flight, with tears in my eyes. Had it reached the camp, already watered our pastures? Had anyone set out to look for me? Would I find my little lost love? Was Mbarka still out there somewhere? The rain offered no answers. It fell more softly now, just a light trickle, but I was already completely soaked. My head ceased to obey me. I could no longer think about the present or the future. I decided to stay in the porch for a while, to gather my strength and wait for daylight to guide me and the sun to warm my body. I was determined not to sleep, though, and I resisted for a long time, but finally my eyelids began to droop. I wrapped my arms around the drum, rested my back against the door and let myself drift away.

I woke abruptly. The door was open and a woman was shouting. I scrambled to my feet. Before I could run, a girl appeared, then a small child, then another girl, then a man. They surrounded me, talking loudly, staring at me. I was paralysed by fear. I couldn't make out their words. I tried to say, 'I haven't done anything, I haven't done anything,' but my voice was inaudible. The woman took me by the arm and pulled me inside. I did not resist. One of the girls reached towards the drum. I hugged it to me instinctively.

Their house was modest but clean, with a well-kept courtyard, two bedrooms and a veranda. A goat skin hung on one wall. 'The poor thing, she's soaked through!' said the woman. At that moment I woke up properly and began to be able to decipher their language. I understood that they were welcoming me. The woman, the children's mother presumably, was around fifty. The two girls were about my age. I was offered dry clothes and a place to change. The woman and the girls spoke quickly and loudly. Their squawking assaulted my ears. They made me lie down on a small mattress and threw a clean cover over me. Still they wouldn't stop talking. My head ached, my voice was gone, and I couldn't answer their endless questions. They placed the drum on a small shelf above me. I imagined it was sounding to call me, and me alone, to tell me I was not finished yet, that I was about to begin a quest that might lead me all the way to the gates of oblivion.

'What's wrong? Are you lost?' 'Where are you from?' 'Are you ill?' 'What do you want to drink?' 'She's tired!' 'She's quite pretty!' 'Her drum is weird!'

My throat was still too hoarse for speech. I could only

make gestures to the effect of, 'God bring you blessings, may Allah reward you!'

They gave me warm milk, scorching hot soup and fresh, sugary dates. Gradually I felt my throat loosen and my energy return. I explained that I'd come from faraway, that I was travelling on a donkey but I'd lost the animal in the storm, that the drum was not mine. To my amazement, they didn't ask for my name or that of my tribe. I babbled that I was Rayhana, of the Oulad Mahmoud. The woman nodded her head and pronounced a heavily-accented *wakhyertt*. The girls' names were Selma and Jemila. They were twins, but they didn't look alike. All the same, I was happy to have met twins the moment I'd arrived in town. My mother had always told me they brought good luck.

I slept for just a few minutes, then woke suddenly. In my dream, a man was pulling me by the hair towards an abyss full of flames, while I argued and screamed. When I opened my eyes, the woman and the girls were standing around me. The mother put her hand on my forehead, told me I had a fever but it would soon pass. The girls leaned over me, curious. The father came in to greet me and ask after my health. He wore a turban with a long end that hung down over his shoulder and amulets around his neck. His coarse white hair surrounded a rough face, the face of someone who had worked all his life.

'How are you feeling now, my child?'

I responded weakly. 'I'm much better. May God reward you!'

'Make yourself at home here. You can stay for as long as you like. At least until you find your family again. The girls will help you.'

He went away. The mother got up too and left me with the twins. They took out pocket mirrors and began to groom themselves. Other girls arrived. They stared at me and asked me questions too. I was tired again already, and didn't always know how to answer them. I stammered a few words. They turned away, looked at their reflections and chattered. I listened to their talk and envied them: their worries were trivial, their hearts did not burn. They spoke of fashion, dresses, veils, shoes, women they'd seen looking beautiful at a ceremony, things that were both insignificant and important. They pronounced foreign names that sounded like a song. They started up a machine that played music of a sort I'd never heard before. It was in our language, using our instruments, mixed with others, but there was something new in it. It didn't sound beautiful, but it did sound modern. One of the girls stood up, wrapped a scarf around her hips and started to dance. The others clapped and swayed to the rhythm. I felt like an intruder in their space. I made myself very small and they forgot about me. Selma poured tea and Jemila put a big plate of *beignets*, bread and groundnuts on the carpet. They invited me to eat. At first I refused, but they insisted. I nibbled a few *beignets* and it felt good. Their laughter and their lightness started to make me feel good too. I imagined myself as one of them, having grown up with them, in the city, far from the privations of the camp. But I also began to recall moments from my childhood that I never wanted to forget. Then I remembered I'd run away, stolen the sacred drum, that my happiness was lost and I had to find it again. I interrupted their joyful game, saying 'I'm looking for a young woman called Mbarka.'

They turned towards me and burst out laughing.

'Mbarka? You're looking for Mbarka?'

Were they laughing because I'd spoken, because I'd interrupted their singing, or because Mbarka was a slave's name?

'Mbarka is like a sister to me,' I said quietly.

'Mbarka what? There are thousands of Mbarkas in this town,' said Selma.

I realised that Mbarka didn't have a surname, had never had one. She was just Mbarka or Mbeirika, her diminutive.

'She's just called Mbarka. She was with us, but she left three years ago,' I murmured.

I stopped talking then, because I felt uncomfortable. They thought I was an idiot, or crazy. I didn't want to be angry, I didn't want to cry. Selma said, without malice, 'we'll go to the market. There are plenty of Mbarkas at Atar market. You can choose your Mbarka.'

The girls hooted with laughter. I tried to join in. I didn't want to upset my hosts, or to seem stupid and over-sensitive.

We left the house. Jemila hailed a battered old car. It stopped in front of us and we all jumped in. I watched as we rushed past houses made of mud and stones, and other, larger ones, like the castles Yahya had boasted about.

'Atar is a big city,' I said thoughtfully. 'There are lots of people living here.'

The girls laughed. 'Atar is a tiny backwater,' said Selma. 'We would never live here if our parents didn't make us.'

When the car stopped, Jemila gave a note to the driver. I was sorry I wasn't able to pay for myself. I'd never had money in my life. I'd sometimes seen my mother counting it or giving it to someone, but I'd never owned it. For us, money was only used to send to the city in return for clothes or food. Only men, or women who were in charge of a household, could have it.

'I'll pay you back one day,' I told Jemila.

'When you sell the drum?' she replied, and they all laughed again. This time I couldn't stop my tears from falling. I suddenly felt weak, lost, insignificant. I didn't know where I was, I knew no one and everything I said made people laugh. I wanted to be somewhere else. Jemila put her arms around me.

'Don't cry! I'm only joking. You turned up at our house. That makes you our sister. Sometimes we might say something to make each other laugh, but you're our sister! OK?'

I nodded and wiped my face, slightly reassured.

The market was a huge space with a circle of stones at its centre, around which people and cars orbited. There were shops everywhere, and, at the back, a building through which crowds of shouting people moved. The stalls and kiosks seemed to go on forever. The air was filled with unidentifiable scents and an incessant hubbub. The noise was deafening. My gaze darted from one thing to another. I didn't know what to look at or listen to first. It was hard to keep up with the twins, who walked at a swift pace, swaying their hips, their bags bumping on their shoulders. Stallholders called out to me, sometimes even grabbed the end of my veil. They said, 'Come and see my beautiful fabrics, henna for your lovely soft feet, taste these *beignets*, this shawl would look wonderful on you, we have excellent ointments, medicine for every kind of pain!' I told them I had no money, apologised and said I was in a hurry. I had to run so as not to lose the twins. They went into a shop which had veils of every colour hanging from its walls. Some designs were simple, others more extravagant, and the materials were exquisite. Jewellery and small boxes containing incense, resins, and other things I didn't recognise were arranged casually on low shelves. A woman sat in the midst of all the merchandise. She didn't get up or reach out to me, but she smiled at the twins. They introduced me. 'She's looking for Mbarka,' said Selma, and they laughed again. I felt ugly, silly and small. I didn't know whether to speak or stay silent. The woman addressed me. 'There are lots of Mbarkas here, but ask around. Maybe you'll find yours.' I got up quickly and left the shop; I felt that was what they wanted me to do. I was angry with myself for having followed the twins, for attaching myself to people I didn't even know. They'd been generous to me, but perhaps it would be better if I left them. Where would I go, though? What if I didn't find Mbarka? I felt panic-stricken, but I decided I should try to find Mbarka alone, rather than stay with people who mocked me. Then I heard Selma calling out, 'Be careful, don't get lost, we'll wait for you!' and I no longer knew what to think.

I ignored the stallholders who called out to me, but walked around examining the merchandise and the people, so many different kinds of people. The variety of things for sale was overwhelming: *boubous*, veils, incense, henna, myrrh, roots, dates, goat skins, butter in little bottles, shoes both old and new... Tailors sat at their machines, flies buzzed around joints of meat and foul-stinking fish, people smiled and called to each other. The walkways were narrow and the merchandise often spread out on the ground. All of it made me dizzy, but I tried to pull myself together, to keep track of where I was going and to try to think. I was here to find Mbarka, the only person who might help me look for my little lost soul. I began to address the people around me:

'I'm looking for Mbarka. I don't know another name for her, she has no family, she's my age, maybe a bit older, she's black, with a mark on her temple, here, she's not very plump, but she's not ugly either, she has difficulty pronouncing her 'r's.'

Some people listened, others didn't even stop. No one knew the Mbarka I described. I tried to find my way back to the shop where the twins were waiting, but I couldn't orientate myself. I thought I was lost, then I heard someone calling my name. I turned and saw Selma coming towards me.

'We've been looking for you everywhere!'

I looked at the ground, incapable of holding back my tears. 'I didn't find Mbarka,' I sobbed when she reached me.

'You'll find her one day.' She put her arms around me. I felt comforted. I don't know why, but suddenly I trusted her.

I spent the evening in bed, my eyes fixed on the drum, which still sat high up on its little shelf, just below the palm trunks that held up the ceiling. I'd hardly eaten anything, despite the insistence of the twins' father, I hadn't washed, or groomed myself as the mother had suggested, and I hadn't gone out with the twins to a party. I'd resisted all their cajoling, their inch'Allahs, their resigned smiles. I stared at the drum. It could read me. I tried to push down the feeling of being overwhelmed, the old images that surfaced. There was no point increasing my suffering by recalling past pain, or crying for what was lost. I had to focus on Mbarka. She was the key; she would help me regain what had been stolen. How to find her, though? The twins would be no use. They were kind but frivolous, and their world was not the same world as my friend's. Nor would their mother be likely to walk the alleyways of the old quarter with me, looking for a young freed slave who meant nothing to her. I couldn't expect any of them to help me. I would have to venture out into the stinking swamp of the city alone.

I was the only person in the camp who knew how Mbarka had left. She told me everything. She'd taken my hand one evening and kissed it. The gesture surprised me.

'I love you very much, little mistress,' she said.

'Mbarka, I'm your friend. It's my mother who's your mistress, and mine too.'

'Rayhana, have you any idea what happens to runaway slaves?'

'Do you mean here or out there?'

'Both.'

'I know they used to cut their hamstrings and stitch their legs inside an animal skin so they couldn't walk, and cut off their ears or their limbs, unless they were going to sell them. That's what my mother told me. These days, sometimes they go after them and get them back, but more often than not they just let them go; and wherever they go, they die of hunger because there's no one to look after them and they're just ignorant beasts. And then life becomes hellish for them because, according to my mother, a slave's paradise is at the foot of his master.'

I spoke playfully. I wanted this to be a game, or a joke. I didn't want to accept or understand.

'I'm leaving,' she said.

'But why Mbarka? Why do you want to leave me?'

'It's not you I'm leaving. It's your mother's camp.'

'But my mother doesn't hit you; she doesn't make you do hard labour. You have a better life than the other slaves. You have good clothes, you eat well. It's true she doesn't like you very much, but my mother doesn't like anyone, except her brother. And if you go wherever it is that runaway slaves go, you'll be poor.'

'Yes, but I can't stay here. I don't want to be a slave. I don't want people to look at me with suspicion, with condescension.'

'Where will you go?

'To the city, to Atar. I've heard that slaves can become free there.'

'I don't want you to leave, Mbarka!'

'I can't stay, mistress! I hate it here. If I don't get away, I think I'll die. Where I'm going, I might go hungry, but I'll have a future. I'll have hope.'

I couldn't understand Mbarka. What happiness could she find in the city? She'd been born amongst us, an orphan. She knew no other family. Why did she need to run away? Where would she run to? According to my mother and my uncle and everyone else in the camp, the city was a magnet for bad spirits and bad people, people with no sense and no soul. Also, I would miss Mbarka. If she went, I'd have no one to talk and laugh with in our tent at night. She was the person I discussed all my joys and fears and dreams with. I didn't want her to leave. In the days that followed, I tried to talk her out of it, to persuade her that her troubles would pass, that soon I would get married and my mother would have no more authority over her. I would take her with me, let her have her freedom and whatever money she needed, then she could go to Atar, or even further if she wanted. I described the horrors of a town I knew nothing about. Mbarka nodded at my clumsy pleading and made no response. She got on quietly with her work and no longer spoke to me about fleeing.

I thought she'd given up on the idea, resigned herself to staying with us. But when she left the house very early one morning and my mother asked me where she was, I answered that she'd gone to the wells, and that afterwards she was going to look for some jewellery I'd lost on the dune, and after that... I went on inventing other things she'd had to do.

No one looked for her. Her name was never mentioned again. Even my mother forgot her. Only I remembered Mbarka, my confidante, my only real friend. That was before the strangers came.

Eventually I stopped brooding and emptied my mind of Mbarka and everything else. The drum danced in front of my eyes; it seemed to come down from its throne towards me. The face of my uncle was etched on to it, then that of my mother, then those of everyone in the camp. I stared at it, waiting for it to swallow me up. It came closer and melted into me. I forgot everything except the drum. It had become me. I heard it beating, shouting, laughing inside me.

I was running through a black night, hugging my little love swaddled in a pure white sheet. Stars fell to earth and exploded in bursts of fire at my feet, trees crashed down behind me and split open with sickening cracking sounds, rocks splintered into fragments before my eyes. The sand opened up to swallow me. I could hear Yahya chuckling, Memed weeping, my uncle cursing me to death, Ahmed Salem promising me hell, my mother calling thunder down on my head. I kept on running, my baby's head pressed against my heart. I did not look back. I leapt over obstacles, jumped as high as the sky and back down again, always hugging my precious burden close. My child stared up at me with black eyes. He opened and closed his tiny fists to tell me he loved me. Suddenly I stopped, breathless, dishevelled, and looked in all directions. I couldn't hear a thing; nature no longer called out to me. The air was filled with silence. I thought I'd won. I opened the sheet to kiss my baby. He had turned into a drum, a tiny little drum.

Day broke and there was nothing; an all-pervading emptiness. Then the voice of the muezzin reached us, familiar and distinct. The grunts of the camels floated freely up to the sky. We could hear buckets of water hitting the sides of wells, babies crying on the other side of the camp. The noises of morning, sounds that had been lost to us, had returned. We stared at each other, amazed. A part of the universe had been silenced. Someone cried out from the top of the biggest dune 'the foreigners!' We didn't understand at first, but he kept shouting, waving his arms, 'the foreigners, the foreigners!' We ran to where he was and were met with a shocking sight: the foreigners' camp was in ruins: spears stood in the ground no longer supporting anything, scraps of rubbish twirled in the breeze. There were pyramids of detritus. The black earth was strewn with torn up planks, empty bottles, ripped tyres, tin boxes with gaping lids. Desolation had settled where once there had been life. We stared at each other for a long moment, then looked back down at the ravaged landscape. Each of us felt a pang: they'd left the same way they'd arrived, without a word, as if we weren't worthy of even the smallest amount of respect, as if we didn't exist. True, we'd ignored each other, but despite everything, we'd been neighbours. It felt like an insult, the breaking of an unspoken pact. Children ran down to the abandoned camp and returned with plastic tubes, iron bars, tins, a small cooking pot, books filled with indecipherable words. The chief ordered that everything be taken from them and burned. The ground the foreigners had camped on had been tainted. The stains they'd left had seeped beneath the soil; the scant bushes that had once grown there were dead. The place was lost for wells or for grazing.

Our imam went down to the camp and recited some suras to expel djinns. The chief announced the place was out of bounds for people or animals for at least a generation. Ahmed Salem exulted, thanking God for sending the heathens away.

The girls were more shocked than anyone by the desertion. We were the only ones with a direct link to the foreigners' camp, in the shape of Yahya. He'd said nothing to us. Just the night before, he'd brought delicious sweets and had sat for a long time, telling stories, reciting poems, laughing uproariously.

My friends looked to me for an explanation. I had nothing to offer them. Not for an instant did I believe that Yahya would abandon me. It was true that the night before he had not slipped between the tents to see me, but I wasn't concerned. He'd be back, a spectre in the gloom, navigating the silent night to come to me and stir up strange emotions.

I stayed awake all night, listening intently, my heart leaping at every whisper of wind, every beating of a flap against the side of a tent, every weary herdsman's cough. The next few nights were the same. My eyelashes quivered from the effort of keeping my eyes open, eyes that were red-rimmed from crying. Finally, I accepted the evidence: Yahya had left without telling me. My stomach clenched in anger, my heart began to crack, I hated the world. I wanted to burn down the tents, wipe the smiles off my friends' faces, shake all the people in the camp out of their stupor. I was incensed with the sun for rising every day, with the imams for continuing to call us to prayer, with the camels for wandering the way they did. Rage bubbled inside me. I'd been used, irredeemably soiled. Love had left me, and I knew then that it had never been love in the first place. The whole thing had been no more than an appeal to my vanity, my desire to obtain the thing all my friends dreamed of, to taste forbidden pleasures. Yahya had just been lonely. He'd needed breasts, a body, a sex. He'd used cunning to steal from me the one thing I'd been taught to refuse. To satisfy his hunger, he'd trampled down my flimsy defences. Yahya was foul, and he'd deposited his pestilence in me. He was like the ass in the legend, who closes up the well as soon as his own thirst is quenched.

For a few days I remained prostrate, incapable of action. I wept, not because of Yahya, who I now hated, but because of my own stupidity. Why had I been so ready to accept his words, words I now saw as meaningless and crude? Why had I allowed myself to be bewitched by his false, laughing eyes, let my awareness become so blunted I'd accepted his intrusion? Was it just to relieve the monotony of my days and nights? Was it because I ached to escape to unknown lands? I had no good excuses; it was foolish even to look for them. I'd relinquished the best part of myself, and not even for love, but out of naivety, credulity and ignorance.

I considered death. I could jump into a well and be destroyed by the fall or perish through drowning. But then the tribe would forbid the well's water from ever being used again. I'd be forcing them into exile. I could steal a gun and shoot myself. But I could see no way to sneak into the warriors' tents, and I wouldn't know how to use the weapon. I might only manage to seriously injure myself, become a vegetable, neither living nor dead, for the rest of my life. I could choose thirst, send myself into exile in the desert, to the north, where there was nothing. But they'd come after me and bring me back. I'd be the laughing stock and shame of the whole camp. I wished I could simply will myself to stop breathing. I tried, but it didn't work.

I no longer saw my friends. Whenever my mother went out, they came to our tent to try to comfort me. I swore it wasn't Yahya I was mourning, only the fact I had believed his lies. I told them I no longer thought about him, but I didn't want to come out because in the day time I had a headache and in the evenings my mother felt unwell and I didn't want to leave her alone. They didn't believe me for a minute, but I didn't care.

Later I would hear them singing and beating the jerry can on the dune, and my tears would flow. Happiness no longer felt possible for me. I couldn't imagine singing and laughing wholeheartedly ever again. Yahya had destroyed my youth and my dreams, and I couldn't even complain: I had no one to blame but myself. My mother heard my sobs. I told her I was suffering from terrible migraines. All she could think of to say was, 'They'll pass.'

The days went by and I forced myself to forget. What was lost was lost. There was no point thinking about the future either: I wouldn't marry, I'd refuse every offer if it was the last thing I did. No one could be allowed to scrutinise my shame. It was a battle I'd just have to learn to fight: every time a spouse was suggested to me, I'd find a thousand excuses. If they forced me, I'd forbid the man from coming to my bed and he'd divorce me. I would do it again and again, until they gave up. Mouna, the oldest girl in our *cadi*[10], was somewhere between twenty five and thirty and still hadn't found a husband. No one asked for her any more, because she was too old. Her parents had given up. I'd be like her, an old spinster that no man wanted. I'd be left in peace. It would be hard, but time would heal me. I only had ten or fifteen years to wait.

My migraines eased, but I'd lost weight. Nothing could engage my emotions or my attention. The stories and legends that had always nourished me now seemed like nightmares, or foolish nonsense. I vowed that now I was free of illusions, fully myself, in control of my own eyes and my own heart, I would learn how to look at the world and understand it properly. I would never be blinded again. My virginity had been taken, but I'd learned the truth that lay behind flattering words. My struggle would now be to rebuild myself, to keep the demons of the night at bay, to resist the lure of death that whispered in my ears.

I sought refuge in religion. I lengthened the time I spent in prayer. Every day I worked my prayer beads, intoning the ninety-nine names of the creator. I visited the camp marabout each day and he wrote out a sura for me on a large wooden tablet, which I took back to our tent. I tried going along with the old women to a religious evening course the teacher was holding, but I soon tired of his lectures: they were hard to understand, and spoke of a world that wasn't ours, names that were not our sheiks, traditions that were alien to us.

10 Translator's note: a Muslim community.

One evening, when I came back from class, I heard my uncle and my mother talking. I hid behind a tent flap to listen.

'Memed is waiting,' my mother said. 'He asked for her hand a few days ago. I can tell he's getting impatient.'

'I know,' said my uncle. 'He keeps walking past me. He's waiting for an answer.'

'So, why don't you answer him?'

'Because I'm still not sure.'

'Why not? Doesn't he seem like a good match?'

'Yes and no. Yes because he's one of our tribe, he's been in the city, even learned foreign languages, his family is rich, his father is a humble, pious man and his uncle is, as you know, the richest man in the region. Memed himself is of very good moral character, and they also tell me he has a good collection of livestock. But his grandfather was a simple herdsman, and his father worked in the city, for others. Those things devalue him a little.'

'So you're going to refuse?'

'I haven't decided. I need to think some more.'

'He's waiting for your answer. He's let me know that quite a few times.'

'He'll have to wait a little longer. I'm not sure what to think. He may not be the best match for your daughter. Also, if I marry her without telling her father, it will be without his consent.'

'But he abandoned us! He declared in public that he rejected everything that connected him to you: his daughter, his possessions, even his tribe!'

'But you know that man. Tomorrow he might appear and kick up a fuss, accuse me of having stolen his daughter.'

'He rejected me, he left her, he's never been back. You're the only person now who can decide, for me and him.'

'I don't want to start a new quarrel with him. In spite of everything, your daughter's father is still her legal guardian. I shouldn't act without his agreement. If I do, he could create a scandal, take it to the tribal assembly. He always accused me of being a bad chief, of over-stepping my authority.'

'But how are we supposed to inform him if we don't even know where he is?'

'He's disappeared into one of the cities, he's chosen poverty and exile, he refuses all contact with us. I don't know! If we can't locate him after a few months, perhaps I can make a decision then, but I'd need to ask for the advice of the *cadi*. I must have the support of the *cadi* or the tribal assembly. My cousin could make a lot of trouble.'

Why had Memed asked for my hand without saying anything to me? Didn't he know I was lost to love and everything related to it?

'That girl,' my mother said, 'is a shadow of her former self. You've seen how thin she's got. I'm worried she's ill.'

'If you like I can send her to a doctor in town.'

'I've never had any faith in *Nçara* medicine.'

'There's old Oumou. She knows plant medicine.'

'I'll call for her.'

Oumou had always frightened me. Long amulets hung from her neck and her hair was knotted together in a dusty weave. Her large eyes had red threads dancing in them. Her voice was harsh. She felt my scalp and my forehead, lifted my eyelids to inspect my pupils, pressed my stomach with her rough hands, then said in a decisive tone, 'This girl is inhabited by bad humours. She has too much bad blood. She's suffering from *iguindi*[11]. If you want her to get better, you'll have to take her faraway, to a village of the Imraguen fish-eating tribe. She should spend two months there, eating the flesh and oil of fish. That will cure her.'

I was happy to make the trip. My camp and my people had begun to oppress me, nothing amused me any more; all I saw were the same faces with the same unspoken questions written on them, the same foreheads lined with the same preoccupations, all revolving around the same things: rain, wells, pastures. The whole camp knew Memed had asked for my hand. They talked of nothing else. I felt eyes following me when I walked past tents, I sensed whispers and read an interrogation in every smile. The distance would allow me to forget, to breathe, perhaps to reclaim the space around me.

Two fine camels were harnessed and saddled for my mother and me. A third carried our bags. Perched up high, sheltered from the beating sun and the blustering wind, I let myself be rocked by the gentle sway of the sedan seat. I gazed, mesmerised, at the smooth undulations of the reddish dunes, and the ever-blue horizon, which seemed to move further away from us all the time. Our guide was Salem, a *znagui*[12] attached to my uncle. He wore a large belt and had a tightly-knotted turban on his head. His *boubou* floated behind him. He

---

11 Author's note: An illness which, according to Saharans, results from too little variety in the diet.
12 Author's note: Belonging to a vassal or subjugated tribe, often guardians of herds.

guided my mother's camel by the reins with one hand, while in the other he held a stick, which he sometimes twirled in the air above his head. He moved briskly, but without rushing. He sang old Saharan tunes and recited ancient poems. A young servant girl, Meylouda, followed behind him, hurrying to keep up. I wasn't sure why my mother had chosen such a puny child to accompany us. It was true she didn't need much help with the domestic chores, and we were only two, but I wished it could have been Mbarka coming with us; Mbarka who was not a servant in my eyes but my best friend, Mbarka who was so full of laughter, so intelligent and kind, Mbarka with whom I shared everything, even my Quran lessons from school. But my mother had never liked Mbarka, and Mbarka had run away.

The scent of the sea reached our nostrils long before we arrived at our destination. We began to take our first lungfuls of ocean breath. I felt a new, soft air caressing my body, completely different from the harsh winds of our territory. I gulped down the surprising scents, fluid and fresh. This sweet air seemed filled with hope, like the air that preceded the rains where we came from, but more constant and more alive. It clung to my whole body. My mother said that when the ocean belched in the afternoon, it settled nature's belly and tamed the spirit. Suddenly I felt ready for serenity and forgetting.

We set up camp an hour's walk from the sea, on flat ground surrounded by dunes. My mother wanted as little contact as possible with the Imraguen fish-eating people. She said they were common and dirty. A listless old woman was sent by the Imraguen village chief to serve us. My mother, already irritated by the playful little Meylouda, sent her away again.

Every morning we got dried fish from the Imraguen village

and ate it with our tea. At midday, we had rice splashed generously with fish oil. In the evenings, we soothed our stomachs with camel's milk, sometimes corn pancakes. The days would pass without a murmur, except that of the wind. My mother pored over her Quran, oblivious to the world around her. I tried to empty myself, to tame the demons that inhabited me, to forget Yahya and my terrible defeat, to refine my arguments for quietly, unobtrusively rejecting Memed on our return. Young Meylouda, with little to do except the occasional small errand to the Imraguen village, spent most of her time playing outside the tent.

Salem, the *znagui*, fetched our water from the nearest well, which was a long way away. He left before sunrise and didn't get back until late at night when we were already asleep. The next day, we were able to refill our goatskins and gourds, have a quick wash with a piece of soap and clean our dirtiest clothes and some utensils. We would have enough water for three days, then Salem would have to leave again. On the days when he didn't go for water, we saw him only early in the morning or in the middle of the night when he milked the camels and brought us the milk. He rarely came inside the tent. His free time was spent in the fishermen's village, where he said he had made good friends.

I went to the Imraguen village only once. It was a place of ramshackle huts, old people with gaunt profiles following you slowly with dull eyes, children with pockmarked faces and protruding stomachs, women with toothless smiles, wearing dirty robes stained with oil, their heads uncovered. The ground was black and viscous and the air smelled of fish. There were scraps of net everywhere, and raw fish hanging outside houses.

I held my nose and got out of there as quickly as I could, thanking God I had been born in a place of wide open spaces, free from vermin.

Every Friday, we went to the sea. It was practically a sacred pilgrimage for my mother: the sea, she said, was an eloquent expression of the omnipotence of God. You could wash away unknown maladies by sprinkling sea water on yourself while invoking the saints. We approached the water only to wet our hands and our feet, then my mother would point at it and murmur an inaudible prayer. We filled a bottle with sea water and took it home for our ablutions. I was surprised that although our tribes sanctified the sea, we had only minimal physical contact with it. My mother said it was because of the salinity of the water. I thought the real reason was the horizon. It disturbed us to see something before us that we couldn't reach. The ocean, unlike a river, couldn't be understood as leading to a destination. We couldn't imagine what was beyond it; maybe it was the land of the djinns, maybe there was a gaping hole, the end of the world, the place where the dead went, hell or paradise. When my mother murmured her suras facing that infinite vastness I imagined human destinies concealed within the folds of the waves, all that had already been and was yet to come. The sea knew everything. The way the waves died on the sand, only a league away from our arid desert, was meant to remind us of the transitory nature of things.

The Imraguen fishermen would beat the sea with clubs fashioned from large stones tied inside long pieces of cloth. They swung them around their heads, then allowed them to crash down on to the bluish water. The water splashed up, flashing like crystal, as if the sea was crying. The beating produced a thick, heavy sound. The Imraguens shouted with rage, the sprays of water shone around them like tears, and I gasped as I saw dolphins appearing, lifting their beautiful noses from the water to greet the fishermen from afar, plunging back into the water, their backs illuminated by a thousand sparkles, then returning to the surface again. The Imraguens held out their nets and hundreds of fish jumped in, generous offerings from the divine dolphins who wanted the sea's suffering to stop. The nets closed on mouths that gasped for life, with a dry slapping sound, like a sob. The gleam of the wriggling fish was reflected on the faces of the fishermen. They cried out in joy. When the nets were full, the dolphins turned round, fins held high, proud to have sated the hunger of the fishermen and healed the wounds of the sea. They could still be seen for a little while, dancing in the distance.

I began to experience nausea, then I started to vomit. I was visibly thinner, and all I could do was sleep. At first my mother put this down to the change of location and climate. Finally she got worried and summoned the Imraguen village healer, an old woman called Massouda. This woman felt my stomach and breasts, examined my teeth and eyes, then addressed herself to my mother. She said cheerfully, 'Your daughter is pregnant!' My mother asked her several times, in a weak voice, to repeat the diagnosis. She turned to me. I thought she was going to kill me there and then. Her face was pale, her eyes rolled upwards and she was trembling all over.

'Is it possible?' she thundered.

I nodded, preparing to disappear.

My mother stood up with difficulty. She let out a short

cry, then swallowed it. She remained immobile for a while, tears running down her cheeks, then I heard her praying in a low voice. This seemed to last for an eternity. I was frozen, incapable of speech. I silently begged the earth to engulf me. I expected the worst and I would accept it. I had never entertained the possibility that I might carry the fruit of my transgression inside me but as soon as the verdict was given, I understood that it was fair and that I would die. The old woman, frightened and tremulous, stared at the two of us. My mother sat down again. She put her head in her hands. Then she stood up, went out of the tent and looked all around her. She returned, and without regarding me once, took Massouda by the arm.

'Woman,' she said, in a voice that was suddenly calm and decisive, 'you are the only witness to my shame. No one else must ever find out. If they do, I swear on the prophet and all the saints that I will make you disappear. I will have you thrown, with your hands and feet tied, into that sea that your nasty tribe adores. All of your relatives will become slaves, faraway, deep in our deserts. Your village will be razed to the ground by our warriors. No one will be able to do a thing, not even the authorities. Do you understand me?'

Her voice had changed, her features had hardened, her face was unforgiving.

Massouda shook. She said, 'I won't say anything, mistress, I swear!'

'You will stay near us,' my mother continued, in the same tone. 'You can go back to visit your people or to heal if you have to, but most of the time you must be with us. You will watch over my evil daughter until she gives birth. No one else will be allowed to go near her. I will give you money, lots of money, as well as a sheep and a camel, but you will say nothing, for as long as you live, or I swear by the prophet, you will no longer see daylight and your children and grandchildren will all become slaves.'

'I won't say anything, mistress,' the old woman repeated tearfully.

I listened without reacting. It was as if my senses were all dead and my brain had emigrated to unknown lands, erasing everything in me. I had become a desert. My mother could kill me, the earth could fall into darkness, the stars disappear, everything be annihilated. My imagination had vanished. I no longer thought about anything, no longer really existed. I languished, awaiting whatever fate had in store for me and caring little about it. Sometimes old stories floated back to me that friends had told in whispered voices; stories of girls who'd committed terrible wrongs and been sent faraway by their parents, never to return; brothers or fathers who'd killed their sisters or their daughters in the name of family honour; newborns buried underground so no one would know. These stories flashed across my consciousness, a string of images. I drew nothing from them, I simply watched them pass. I was a slack body, indifferent and incapable of response.

My mother created a force field around us. Our tent was forbidden to everyone from that moment onwards. Salem would place the goatskins of water and the milk in front of it and leave as quickly as possible. It was old Massouda who went to the Imraguen village to get the things we needed. My mother told the servant girl Meylouda that she was good for nothing except for annoying us. She hired a camel driver to take the girl back to our camp and to tell my uncle we'd settled well and were going to lengthen our trip. I no longer left the tent except to go to the toilet, followed closely by old Massouda, who had become my shadow.

I began to feel a new heaviness, new twinges in my body, abdominal pains. My stomach was growing. I didn't touch or look at myself. It was as if the pains weren't mine, had nothing to do with me. I was inhabited by someone else. I hadn't asked for this; all I'd done was accept words and caresses, followed by a pleasure which I'd neither expected nor requested. I remained dazed, desiring nothing except to be rid of my unwanted burden and sink into oblivion.

Massouda proved to be a caring, thoughtful woman. She enveloped me with affection, always calling me 'my child'. She tried to lift my spirits, to coax smiles from me. She spent all day telling me stories and repeating to me that I had my life ahead of me, that to make a mistake was not to die. In the evenings, when I cried, she took me in her arms and rocked me like a baby.

My mother no longer looked at me or addressed a single word to me. She gave Massouda orders concerning me, referring to me as 'the other one', or 'my curse.' Her contempt was clear in her voice, in the way she grimaced, in the glances she threw in my direction. Every time she referred to me I wanted to bury myself in the ground and cease to exist.

In the rare moments that my lucidity returned, I seriously considered ending it all, but I was too well guarded, and I didn't seem to have the energy even for death.

I was angry with Atar for not really liking me. I felt no friendliness in either the winding alleyways of the old quarters or the wide avenues of the new parts of town. The streets were always crowded, but no one showed the slightest interest in me. I wondered whether I existed at all. It was true I was still wary of my tribe, so I only appeared in public well covered, in a veil that hid half my face. But I didn't hesitate to approach passers-by to ask them about Mbarka. Some replied, 'Good luck, there's no shortage of Mbarkas!' laughing at their own joke. Others told me about Mbarkas that bore no resemblance to mine. Some people just stared, as if amazed to see me standing in front of them, then walked away.

I left the twins' house early every morning and explored the city alone. I walked the whole length of the *batt'ha*, the river of sand punctuated by palm trees, then meandered through the alleys of the kasbah. I was amazed by the large stone structures overhanging the road, which seemed to have nothing holding them up, by the labyrinthine paths, all of which lead to the mosque, by the unidentified ruins and the new houses with garish facades. Sometimes I cast furtive looks through open doors. I got lost in the warren-like old city, then found myself again, without knowing how. I went to the market place, crossing the big circle of stones they called the '*poinronh*'[13] swiftly, to avoid meeting the twins and their friends; they would laugh at my quest and I would waste too much time talking to them. I visited Ghanemritt, Barka Amara and Kanawal. I found nothing, and no one could offer me any assistance. City people, it seemed, were not in the habit of speaking to each other in the streets. They rushed around, whether on foot, by car, or by bicycle, without a backwards glance. They walked quickly, like a herdsman tracking a lost animal. When I approached them, the response was always a quick 'no'. Those who weren't in a hurry sometimes listened and smiled, probably thinking me crazy. Others were indignant to see a girl who, despite her old clothes, seemed to be from a good family, asking after a Mbarka. Young men sometimes flirted with me. The children I approached did not return my smile or take the hand I extended. They retreated, their little foreheads creased. I wished I had dates or small gifts to offer them, but I had nothing. They fled, garbling incomprehensible words.

Atar and its people didn't like me. They stared, amused, as if I'd dropped from the sky, or arrived from some bizarre foreign land. They whispered and sniggered. I understood them well enough: they were saying, 'She's a Bedouin!' I replied inside my head, 'So what? do you think I'm ashamed of that? Do you think I'd rather have what you have? Your grimy faces, your vacant eyes, your directionless lives, the prisons you live in, the dead things you use for transport? Do you think you're better than me? You don't stop to talk, you don't even greet people you pass, you're so desperate to survive that you never experience life!' I began to feel more and more disdain for

---

13 Translator's note: 'point rond' (roundabout).

the town and everyone in it. People seemed to have forgotten what they'd been only yesterday, what their fathers and their fathers' fathers had been. They were content to no longer be nomadic, to no longer feel the sun on their heads. They were happy to eat new dishes made not with their own wheat or barley, or with the meat or milk of their own animals. They were proud of all that; they thought it meant they could look down on those of us who had stayed as we were, who hadn't succumbed to the temptations of the new. Sometimes I would sit down, exhausted, in the shadow of a wall, to get my breath back before continuing my quest. Passers-by sometimes offered me a coin. I would immediately throw it back in their faces. But if a house door opened and a woman invited me in to rest and have a drink, I always accepted. I was a guest then; it was not charity but hospitality, a gesture from the heart that couldn't be bought or sold. Those who invited me in were always recent arrivals to the city, still faithful to the old ways. They would give me a bowl of *zrig,* milk mixed with cold water. When I'd drunk my fill, they'd pour me tea. Often I shared meals with these generous people too.

Once I came upon a group of foreigners strolling through the streets. I wondered if they might be the same ones who'd been near our camp. I approached their guide and he asked them for me. 'They don't know what you're talking about,' he replied. I hardly heard what he said: I'd become spellbound by the face of a blond, curly haired child. His mouth was daubed with some black thing he was licking. His mother held his hand and reprimanded him in a forceful, guttural language. I couldn't resist approaching the child, smiling, reaching out my hand to touch his cheeks. They looked so soft I wanted to kiss them. The mother gave me a murderous look. The guide hurled insults at me and threatened to call the police. I moved away quickly.

In the afternoons I returned to my hosts. They were shocked by what they referred to as my absconding. The mother scolded me gently, the girls wanted to know where I'd been, and had I found my Mbarka? I never replied. I went to the room where the drum was kept, sat down opposite the relic and addressed it in a low voice, 'Another joyless day of wandering, another day in which I remain an orphan because of what you stole from me. But you too are alone, rejected, unrecognised, forgotten. You no longer sit proudly between the two spears that supported you outside the chief's tent. Your glory days are over. I'm the only one in this whole ignorant city who knows you; all they see is an ordinary tom-tom, cow skin and wood. They have no idea you're the *rezzam*, the bugle that used to proclaim the tribal pride of the Oulad Mahmoud. They don't know that our marabouts blessed you, that their sacred cowrie shells are tucked inside you, they have no idea that our warriors obey you blindly. There you lie, next to the plain furniture of ordinary people. I stole you to strangle the vanity you represent, a vanity that has condemned me to exile and misery. There you'll remain, a prisoner, humiliated, crushed, far from everything that's yours, until they've endured what I've had to endure, until I find the life they stole from me. Without you, they will no longer be able to hold their heads high and shamelessly rob people of their hearts and souls.'

One evening, the sounds of the *med'h* and the *bendje* floated towards me from somewhere nearby. I was gripped by an old nostalgia for those passionate songs and boisterous dances. I'd watched them, fascinated, in front of the slave tents, on evenings when I'd disobeyed my mother and followed Mbarka out. Something inside me was straining to be released: I felt an irrepressible urge to dance.

I went into the street. I could see no signs of a gathering. The sounds of singing, the beating of tom-toms and the clapping of hands floated upwards, only to be swallowed by the muggy air of that rainy season evening. Listening intently, I managed to work out which direction the sounds were coming from. I hurried through the dark streets for several blocks until I reached a tall door in front of which a small crowd had gathered. I ducked under arms, squeezed between bodies and sneaked through. I found myself in a large courtyard bustling with people. There was a stage on which a band, made up of men and women, was playing. The men wore blue *boubous* and white turbans. The women, mostly old, wore bright blue haïks[14]. Their song alternated a verse of a *med'h* with one of a *bendje*. This was strange to me. The *med'h* of slaves is a powerful music in which strident voices sing of their love for the prophet and the trials and tribulations of daily life. It's an expression of the faith of simple people. As an evocation of God and the prophet, it's not for dancing, more for listening to, perhaps clapping along to. The *bendje*, on the other hand, is an expression of joy, with fevered melodies that excite the instincts and emotions, and lyrics that can be suggestive and crude. The *bendje* is for dancing to, for opening your legs, thrusting out your chest, shaking your bottom. It's a dance forbidden to girls from good families. If the *med'h* describes the spirit entering

---

14 Translator's note: a robe that covers the whole body.

the soul, the *bendje* is the devil seizing the body. The way this band conflated the two disturbed me at first. Then I got used to it, and the fever began to take hold, not just of me, but of everyone around me. Before I knew it, I was jiggling about in front of complete strangers, a long-forgotten warmth coursing through me, a burden lifting from my shoulders, a lightness inhabiting me until I forgot everything; my escape from the camp, my anger, even my lost love. I became only my movements; head and arms raised to the sky, chest and belly quivering, the world twirling around me in a frenzied spiral and me following wherever it went. At the point when my thoughts had been completely silenced, when I was nothing but an enraptured body, I suddenly felt myself gripped by two arms. Someone was shouting my name. I opened my eyes and at first saw nothing. Then, through a dizzy blur, I saw the face of Mbarka. I was speechless. I stopped dancing and dropped to the floor.

Mbarka put her arms around me. She murmured in my ear, 'I'm here, little sister, it's me, little mistress.' She led me to the side of the crowd, took hold of my arms and looked me up and down. Her voice caught as she said, 'How beautiful you've become, little mistress! God has put flesh on your bones. You're no longer a skinny little girl; you're a ravishing young woman! But what are you doing here? Has your family come to Atar?'

'No, Mbarka, I'm alone.'

'Alone?'

'Yes. I've run away from the camp.'

Mbarka stared at me, open-mouthed.

'I hate my people: my uncle, my mother, all of them. I fled,

Mbarka. I spat on them and everything they believe in. They stole the fruit of my womb, my little love, Mbarka, and in return I've stolen their drum. To punish them for their stupid vanity, to castrate them, to shame them.'

Mbarka was stupefied.

'I've stolen their pathetic totem, do you see? Their pride and joy. They're chasing me and I'm running from them, and looking for the little soul they snatched away from me.'

Mbarka was still staring at me, wide-eyed. She glanced to left and right, afraid someone might be listening. She thought I was crazy.

'I'm not crazy, Mbarka. I'm fine. But I have suffered. I've been looking for you everywhere.'

Mbarka didn't answer. She pressed her lips together, fixed me with her eyes, still incredulous.

'Where are you staying?' she asked finally.

'Some good people took me in.'

'Listen,' she said, speaking very quietly, trying to control her emotions, 'you'll come with me.'

'Yes. But I'll go back to my hosts' house first.'

'You have things there?'

'The drum.'

'The drum? No, no! If it's true that you took it, it would be best to lose it.'

'Never!'

'It will be the death of both of us!'

'If you won't have me with the drum, then I won't come to you.'

'Be reasonable, Rayhana. This is all very hard for me to understand. I don't have any connection with your camp

75

any more. I've no idea what they did to you. I'm sure you'll explain it to me. But I know they would kill us for that drum.'

'I won't come to your house without the drum.'

Mbarka led me even further away from the crowd. 'Rayhana, I love you very much. I don't know if you're in your right mind, but I sense that you did something wrong. I don't know what it was, but it must have been serious, and you must have suffered. I can well imagine that. But to steal the sceptre of the tribe? It's insane! No rebel, no freed slave ever even contemplated it. They'll definitely come looking for you. We can't keep the drum with us. Leave it with your hosts, tell them what it is so they can tell the tribe and they can come and get it back. Then perhaps they'll leave us alone. And when you've made peace with your mother and your uncle…'

'You haven't understood a thing, Mbarka. I've left them all, forever. I'll never go back to the camp!'

Mbarka looked one way and then the other again. Then she sat down on the floor.

'You're making my head spin, sister. I don't know what to think.'

She fixed her eyes on a point in space that I couldn't see. Suddenly she seemed lost, close to tears. Was she thinking about her past, her suffering, the trouble I was bringing her now?

'Don't worry, Mbarka,' I said. 'I don't want to be a burden to you. I'll stay with my hosts till I've had time to think. Then I'll leave, and find my own way.'

'No, sister, I won't leave you again. I don't know what we're going to do, but I won't leave you. You'll explain it all to me, then maybe I'll understand. Go and collect your drum, and your other things if you have them. Do your hosts know about me?'

'I've spoken to them about Mbarka.'

'There are hundreds of Mbarkas in this town.'

'They know you were with us at the camp.'

'That's OK. Atar is full of slaves who've run away from the oases and the camps. They shouldn't see me though. I'll wait for you here.'

I ran back to my hosts' house. I gave the mother a tender kiss on the cheek. 'May God reward you with a long life,' I said. 'May the angels of abundance surround you, may sorrow always keep its distance. I've found the sister I was looking for. I'm going to go with her.'

'What, my child? You're leaving us?'

'Yes, mother, but I'll never forget you. I'll come to see you often. I'll go and kiss the girls and then I'll leave.'

'Those bird-brains are out. Won't you wait till they get back?'

I wasn't sorry the twins were absent. They would ask too many questions.

'No, mother, I must leave straightaway. May peace accompany you everywhere!'

I went into the room and took the drum in my arms. 'You go with me wherever I go,' I told it. 'You're my hostage, mouthpiece of all the idiocies that led to my destruction. You'll accompany me on my wanderings, be beside me in exile, share my long nights of worry and pain. As soon as I find my child, I'll let you go. You can return to them then if you like, go back to propping up their outdated beliefs. Come on, tired symbol of their idolatry, come with me!'

The mother embraced me again. She pressed some notes into my hand.

'This will help.'

I couldn't refuse. I knew the family were poor, and the crumpled notes came straight from the heart.

Mbarka was waiting. She held open the door of an old taxi. She took the drum from me, weighed it in her hands, then gave it back. She couldn't believe it.

'It really is the *rezzam*,' she said quietly. 'The *tombol*!'

She put the drum in the back of the taxi and invited me to get in. She pointed to the driver.

'That's Khattri.'

'You're married now, Mbarka? Do you have a pretty baby?'

It was Khattri who answered me, laughing. 'I'm not her husband, nor am I a pretty baby!' Mbarka and I laughed too. She looked at me with her lips pressed together, then she shook her head and examined me more closely, as if to assure herself it was really me.

'I still can't believe it, Rayhana, I still can't believe it,' she repeated.

I was silent. She grabbed my hand. 'I've thought about you so much over the years. I've always wondered what happened to my little mistress, so pretty and bright. I knew you were different: a nice girl who would become a tigress if she was ever wronged too deeply.'

'I've been crushed, Mbarka,' I responded feebly. 'I'm dead.'

'You're not dead. Here you are, telling me about it.' She rapped my knuckles.

I knew then that she would accept me, whatever madness

I'd committed, that she was on my side. I tried to hold back my happy tears; I didn't want to cry in front of a man I didn't know. Now I had Mbarka, I was no longer an intruder in the city. I had eyes that did not regard me with amusement or pity, ears that would listen properly to what I had to say, arms that would support me. I was no longer helpless and lost. Perhaps now I'd be able to find some moments for myself. And perhaps Mbarka would know where to look for my little lost love.

Mbarka's home was three inter-connected rooms with a large sandy courtyard in front. The courtyard was clean and bare, with just the one goatskin of water hanging on spears. We went into one of the rooms, apparently the spare bedroom. It was furnished with a simple rug and some low mattresses on the floor. Khattri left us. Mbarka explained that he was just a friend; a friend in the way it was meant in town, not a partner. She bolted the door behind us, saying, 'No one's coming in tonight.'

We sat down. Mbarka prepared tea. 'I'm listening,' she said. 'I want to understand.' I wasn't sure how to begin. Words made their way to the tip of my tongue, then melted away. Images merged and overlapped in my brain. The pain of remembering stopped me short. It was as if I was weighing it in my hands. Now that I was preparing to describe my troubles, I saw and felt them differently. I distanced myself from them, but only so as to feel them more completely. At the same time, part of me wondered if it was all true. Had these things really happened?

Mbarka fixed her eyes on my face, as if she was trying to bore through it into my brain, to mount the horses of my words and ride right inside me. She wanted to be me, but only I could be me. I'd scaled the sand dunes of suffering alone, gone right to the top. I knew whatever happened in the future would be bearable, because I'd already survived so much. As I told Mbarka my story, I imagined it was someone else talking, telling an old tale devised to make young girls cry, nothing to do with me.

Mbarka didn't interrupt or ask any questions. Sometimes she looked down and wiped away a tear. When I'd finished, we both sat still for a while. Then she got up and left the room without a word. She was gone for a whole hour. I heard a fire being lit, a meal being prepared, some rummaging around. Finally she appeared with a piece of folded fabric in her hands. She laid it in front of me. Inside were some earrings, two gold bracelets and a pair of shoes.

'I haven't touched them,' she said. 'They're the offerings of my liberty, the things you gave me a few days before I escaped. I could never use them as you meant me to because I couldn't bear to separate myself from them. I wouldn't exchange them for my life. They were all I had of you, of the only real friendship I'd ever had.'

'I never expected you to keep them!'

'You must've had to pretend you'd lost them.'

'That's what I said to my mother.'

'Did no one go looking for me?'

'No. You know my mother; she has trouble conceiving of the concept of rebellion. She thought you'd gone to the well, then that you'd gone to look for lost jewellery, or a lost camel. She was expecting you back at any time. A whole day went by like that. By the next day, there would've been no point going after you, you would already have reached one of the towns, "The places where slaves find freedom... and penury," as my mother liked to say.'

'It's not over, sister,' said Mbarka. 'Your quest will be a long one. I'll help you. You were right to steal the thing they adore, right not to believe their lies, right not to dry your tears. I suffered a lot because of being an orphan, having a mother who died when I was a baby, before I got a chance to know her, never experiencing what it was to have a mother. I used to think about her a lot. I know she lived destitute and ignorant, that she was treated like an animal, never educated, not even in the basics of her masters' faith, its God, its rules. She worked all day, and at night her body was available to whoever wanted it, master or slave. She didn't belong to herself, she was orphaned from herself. People always told me I was luckier than her, because your mother picked me. But I was never going to herd camels or cultivate the land. Your mother wasn't the worst mistress. She had disdain for lowly people, and she was taciturn and proud, as you know, but she never laid a finger on me. She never made me do hard labour. I played with you, I wore your dresses, we ate from the same bowl. I even came to the Quranic school with you when you whined and demanded to have me with you. Compared to the other slaves, I was privileged.

It was just that one day I discovered I had a heart that pounded, for me, that my blood was my own blood, that I couldn't bear to remain your mother's property forever. I made the decision one evening while I was dancing with the other slaves, exhausted, trying to keep up with the rhythms of the *bendje*. There was no thunder clap, the sky didn't fall in; I just decided I was going to belong to myself. You were the only person I spoke to about it. I loved you, and I didn't want to betray you. I took the jewels you gave me and prayed to God I wouldn't have to sell them. I was poverty-stricken for months. I was a maid for a few different families, but they always dismissed me after a few days because I was a Bedouin who knew nothing. I lived either with my employers or in the street. Then I met a poor old woman who let me stay in her hovel, out of generosity and pity. Fatmouha treated me like a daughter; she became the mother I'd never known. She offered me love and protection, and gradually I learned how to live here. I began to understand the customs, the way city people think and behave. I like this place, and its people. They're different from what I knew before, but I like the way they accept you. Where you come from doesn't matter. I started to work selling mint in the market. I'd get up at dawn, go to the fields at the edge of town, collect the mint from the peasants and re-sell it at a very small profit. I hailed passers-by, ran behind cars. I lost some of my fear, began to relax, to see the world as it is: it smiles at you if you can forget the past and smile yourself. A smile can heal anything. I always felt detached, I was always excluded from the pleasures I saw other people enjoying every day: brightly coloured veils, shining beads and pendants, fancy hairstyles, make-up, confident expressions, cars... all the casual wealth some people wear like glittering tiaras. And of course I was alone. I had no friends or relatives. There was an emptiness around me. I was a tiny nothing at the centre of a fast-moving whirlpool that could've sucked me down at any time. Then I met a very sweet soul called Hama. He bought mint from me and let me keep the change. He thought I was intelligent and took the time to talk to me. He told me I had no manners but a promising face, that there was a beautiful woman hiding inside me. I was alarmed by him at first, by his effeminate gestures, the idea that he was a *gordiguène*, as they call them here, a homosexual destined for the flames of hell. But I got used to that. One day he invited me to the house he rented and told me he was going to make me beautiful. I learned to be seductive, to speak and laugh with people. It was a thrill. I dived into the only world that would accept me. It's a world I won't talk to you about, except to say that yes, I am a woman of ill-repute, as it's known. My friends and I try to maintain certain standards, we don't accept just anyone, we receive our clients in a living room. It's modest, but we drink tea together, we allow the men to court us, to give us presents and money, before we end up in bed. We're all people who've never had anything, so we play at life. We receive guests, we dance, we sing, we have parties, anything that helps us not to think, to forget ourselves and the world around us. It's a world I won't allow you to be part of. That will be a challenge because my house is small, but you'll stay here, in this room, and I'll live my life in the living room, or in the courtyard if it gets too hot. I'll give you as much of my time as I can. I'm lost, sister, I admit it, but I can't be blamed. Didn't my mother give herself to the first person who came along? And in spite of it all, I'm free. I taste forbidden things because once I was forbidden from living at all. I try to enjoy all the wild flavours that come my way; I taste them with my entire body, with all of my senses.'

Mbarka took me by the shoulders and gave me a little shake, as if to usher away any hidden curiosity I might have for the life she'd described. 'None of this is relevant to you, sister. The gates of my world are closed to you. You're different and you must remain different. Everyone has their own path.'

Mbarka didn't open the door to her friends that evening. We stayed inside and she carried on consoling me and telling me about the city.

I managed to evade Massouda's vigilance. I waited until very late, got up as if to go to the toilet, then disappeared into the misty night. I closed my eyes and walked in the direction of the sea, following the distant sound of the waves. My thin robe floated around me, lifted by the breeze. My uncovered hair, tousled from sleep, fell into my eyes. My legs cried out in pain, as if they'd forgotten how to walk. In my belly I felt the first twinges of the suffering to come. I ignored the discomfort; I was anticipating the joy of bathing my wounds in the deep sea. I walked for a long time, breathless, doubled up in pain, my hands stretched out in front of me, ready to grab the reins of the horses of foam that would carry me out, into the mist, that would lick the gaping wounds on my body with their white spray. Eyes closed, I focussed all my energy on dragging my crumpled form towards the blue expanse ahead.

The sea retreated from my embrace. I needed it, but it rejected me. I longed for it to envelop me in its folds, to wash away the secret pains and injuries I nursed, to erase my troubles with a swish of its waves, to swallow my misery into its depths. Away from the shore, I might have become myself again: alive, free of the interminable heaviness in my belly and my head, free of my crushing solitude and my visions of death. I wanted to open my eyes again and find myself as I was before.

But the sea would have nothing to do with me. I ran towards it, but it ran away. I could hear the thundering of its waves, its rough voice hailing the whole world and all its inhabitants, the songs of the mermaids who came out from the shadows every night, on to the sand, to cry for the fate of humanity. Something was waiting for me out there, arms that would rise up from the water and drag me down into its silence. But I saw only the dunes, the leaves of the acacias swaying in the wind, the tops of the eucalyptus trees shimmering in the moonlight. The quicker I went, the more the sea retreated. It refused to wait. I stopped to catch my breath. My heart hammered, my belly cramped. Then the roar of the waves echoing on the sand summoned me again, and I continued on my desperate course, eyes squeezed shut.

Suddenly, pain coursed through my entire body. I couldn't take another step. The sea now roared inside my belly and my back; agonising waves invaded me, twisting like red-hot pincers. I collapsed on to the sand, my hand on my stomach, and cried out to the sky and the sea to help me. They did not hear. A foul smell filled my nostrils: the stench of death. I roared insults at death as its claws tore at me, sending spasms of pain through my body. Death swirled inside me until I screamed. Moments ago I'd yearned to embrace it; now I tried to push it away with all my strength. I vomited it out. A dark veil shrouded my spirit and I wept with suffering and fear. The sky watched, impassive. I heard voices calling my name. I tried to get up and run again, but I didn't have the strength to move forward. Through the haze of pain, I saw Massouda and my mother rushing towards me, their arms full of things.

They picked me up and laid me on a sheet. My mother wept for her stolen honour while Massouda massaged my stomach and told me to push. I didn't want it to come out, the seed of that beast, the fruit of my abuse. It wasn't me, I didn't do anything, mother, I was just frightened, mother. I forgot everything. I cried again, begging death to take me this time, but Massouda responded with her own cries. She hit me in the face and insulted me, 'Push, you imbecile, push, you fool, unless you want to die!' My mother was at my head now, and she too was begging me not to die, 'Push, my child! We'll put everything behind us, please don't die! Push!' I made a superhuman effort, and in the midst of terrible convulsions, I felt the thing escape.

At first only Massouda paid any attention to the newborn. I stared, stunned, at the mass of flesh that clung to me. Its cries seemed to come from elsewhere, but they appeared to be addressed to me. I obeyed, numb, as Massouda guided me to explore the thing. I looked at his half-closed eyes, his quivering fists that searched my chest, his tiny, puny body, wracked by spasms. I gave him a name, Marvoud – 'the rejected one' – because no one wanted him, not even me. My mother said not a word to me and kept her distance from the baby. She refused to recognise the bizarre name I'd given him, and called him Mohamed, because, 'All illegitimate children should have the name of the prophet. Only he can intercede on behalf of their parents when the final judgement comes.'

My mother increased her vigilance. Even the herdsman, Salem, was no longer allowed to come near our tents. He left the milk very faraway and Massouda had to go and get it. Lost nomads who wandered anywhere close by were warned off with loud shouts, as if our tents had been afflicted with leprosy. My mother wanted the child to remain completely hidden. I no longer felt sick, but I still felt lost. It was as if I was at the edge of a well and couldn't decide whether to jump into it to my death or to quench my thirst with its water. I knew the decision would come soon: my mother would have to choose whether to send me and the child away or to keep us with her. I was prepared for humiliation, for my life to be made hell, for disapproving looks at the camp, insults from other mothers, laughter and finger-pointing from children; or for wandering the desert, babe in arms, or becoming a slave to the Imraguens, or joining the hordes of beggars in the new cities.

The colour gradually returned to my cheeks. Massouda smiled. She made me wear a clean veil and dab some kohl around my eyes. In the evenings we sat outside the tent together, under the stars. She sang old tunes that brought me close to tears. They made me picture a world where happiness could exist, where there were no ogres to devour hearts, where virgins were not delivered to monsters, where it was possible to make a mistake without being shamed, where babies always had a home. I would shake my head to dismiss these crazy thoughts. Just occasionally, a smile would unexpectedly cross my lips, or I would make a joke, even laugh out loud, when speaking to the baby or listening to Massouda. Tiny moments of forgetting, glimmers of happiness that managed to sneak in through the chinks, nothing more.

Massouda told me about the Imraguen fishermen, about their strategies for protecting themselves against sea djinns and for taming them, about how they saw themselves as married to the sea, the wind, the pelicans and the dolphins.

'Our *saleh*[15], Sheikh Bouh, entered into marriage with the sea on behalf of all Imraguens. We love the sea, we know her, when she's unhappy, when she's angry, when she's smiling and when she opens her arms to us. We haven't built boats to travel across her, because why should we travel on the back of the sea? We believe that if you cross to the other side, you never return: the water swallows you up. Without the earth beneath you, you have no roots, no tribe, no heart. It's the end of the world. Monsters open their gaping jaws and devour you. And the djinns, our eternal enemies, are always waiting.

We live beside the sea without violating her. We know her purpose and what she can give to us. We always give her her due, it's an old contract we made together. We take only what's ours and we give back what belongs to her. You must never cheat the sea. If you do, she'll have her revenge; she'll take your child, or carry your men away. Never cheat the sea!

In the beginning, there was the sky, the sea, and the pelicans. They watched our ancestors, the first Imraguens, people who had left their tribes and their clans, who no longer had camels or wells or land. These people were dying of thirst. They were good people. So the sky, the sea and the pelicans decided to help them.

The sky liberated the Great Bear, and the sea, caressed by the winds, brought mullet, whole shoals of them. The pelicans called the dolphins, who were their friends and obeyed them in everything. Together they drove the mullet towards the coast, where the people were waiting. That was how our ancestors were freed from the desert and from hunger. We've learned to

---

15 Author's note: Saint.

do the job of the pelicans ourselves, by hitting at the sea to call the dolphins, and now the dolphins are our friends too. Every season they sing for us, and we organise festivals in their honour. In the summer, when they sometimes get beached on our coasts, we rescue them, splashing water on their bodies so they don't dry out, as you do for the thirsty, then dragging them gently back to the sea. We dive in with them to help them swim past the first waves. The dolphins are our brothers.'

Massouda told me of the war the marabout Bouh had declared against the djinns when they tried to chase the Imraguens from the coast, and of how their talismans could vanquish the spells of 'those we dare not name.'

She told me of the sharks who fell in love with young Imraguen girls, came to cry for them on the beaches and ended up dying of grief, of the brave Imraguens who battled with sea hydras to fish for mullet faraway, courageous sons of the sea who risked their lives to drop a beautiful offering of mullet at the feet of their beloved.

The real world returned to reclaim its rights. Marvoud began to smile at me, and I saw the world in his toothless gums. I learned to amuse myself with him, to tickle him, to laugh when he laughed. As time passed, the weight of my transgression grew lighter. Marvoud's existence drew a line under it all. The birth of my son had taken me to a new place, a place beyond the resentment of an abused young girl. I was prepared to fight for him, to bare my teeth and nails for him, to die to protect him. My mother had closed herself off. She maintained an outraged silence, with just the occasional murmur. She gave Massouda her orders through gestures, and practically never spoke to me. In the evenings I heard her praying to God to save her, to cleanse the impurity from her heart, to wash the stains from her name. I no longer knew whether it was she or I who had sinned. I prayed too, silently, for my mother to recover her lost serenity.

The days passed like this, the sun appearing every morning to lick the earth with its scalding tongue, before handing over, as evening fell, to cool breezes. We were cradled by the smooth passage of night and day. Nothing disturbed the slow, silent march of time. Beyond the flaps of our tent, the world had stopped. I didn't count the hours; they were dead to me, just as all hope of a real life was dead.

Massouda, previously so talkative, now only spoke to the baby, very quietly, as if she was warning him privately of the ills of the world. She rarely went out; when she did it was only briefly. My mother remained cloistered inside her tent. I no longer saw her, didn't even dare poke my head out when she left to go to the toilet or to make sure no one was approaching. We were three prisoners, waiting wordlessly for our sentence.

It was Massouda who came to tell us: a new camp had set up just a few leagues away. The news woke my mother from her lethargy. Perhaps we would have to move. She sent Massouda to gather information. My old friend arrived back trembling, eyes wild. She said in hushed tones, as if enemy ears could hear us, 'They're Tekats! Slave catchers, sellers of souls, pillagers, possessed by the djinns of destruction, impiety and anger, blind to all that is holy, widow and orphan makers! And large numbers of them, a whole tribe I think!' Massouda was merely repeating the traditional view of this tribe. I wasn't afraid: the sudden appearance of ferocious nomads didn't bother me; maybe it would even break the terrible stalemate between my mother and me. I dared to hope that some sort of deliverance might come: something would happen, and the mirror that reflected my days back at me would finally smash. My mother didn't seem concerned either. 'I know that tribe well,' she told Massouda. 'Their camels are ugly, but they're faster than gazelles. Their people have verses on their lips and curses in their hearts, but they know how to receive a guest, how to make a passing traveller feel welcome. They'll raze a camp or an oasis to the ground, vanquish the proudest warrior, test the faith of the marabout, but they'll offer the fruits of their raids to satisfy a guest's hunger. They have no real chief, no emir or nobility, they obey nothing and nobody. Each camp, each *ghazi*[16], chooses one guide; the oldest, or the greediest, or the bravest, or the ugliest, you never know why or how they've been chosen. They follow that person for a season or so, then they choose another. Every *ghazi* has its own way of organising, its own priorities, its own victims too. Some only attack warrior tribes, others attack rich marabout tribes, some go after caravans, others plunder oases, some capture slaves and exchange them for goods, faraway in the Noun *wadi*, usually, or in Tindouf. Others hardly bother themselves with human merchandise and hate ostentatious wealth: they consider gold to be cursed and never touch it. They even pray every evening, I'm told, to be freed from the desire for luxury or beauty, a weakness they distrust. Unlikely though it may seem, they're also excellent poets. But those were the Tekats of old. Today, they suffer the hardships of the modern world,

---

16 Author's note: More commonly called *rezzous*.

like the rest of us: their proud heads have been bowed by laws and bureaucracy. They're peaceful nomads with huge pastures. Their legend lives on, so people are still scared of them, but they're faithful allies of our family. I believe we even have a common ancestor. I'll go and welcome them.'

Massouda, still trembling, went with my mother. I remained alone in the tent, the baby in my arms. It was the first time he and I had been alone together. The idea of running away crossed my mind. I could set out with him on the road to who knows where, in search of tranquillity, a place where there was only happiness and love. We would surely be guided from on high, for we were innocents. The Sahara would take pity on us and not pierce us with its burning arrows, the sky would throw us drops of rain to quench our thirst, then cover us with shade. God would send us beautiful camels to nourish us. We would wander together, a benevolent hand reaching down from the heavens to stroke our heads and offer us sweet shade and all the fruits of Eden. I longed to embrace this ridiculous vision, but I soon snapped out of the fantasy. How could I ever really escape? The immense desert is actually a tiny place: every step bears the name of its owner, every presence tells its story.

When they got back, Massouda told me all about their visit to the Tekats and my mother's meeting with their chief. 'When we got to the camp,' she said, 'they were still setting it up. The women were putting up the tents, the men helping by pulling on the cords to tighten them. Some naked children were chasing a deer, young boys were playing leapfrog, slaves were preparing a meal in a huge pot. There were warriors strolling around, chatting, with guns or sabres on their backs. I was frightened, my child. I swear the place smelled of blood. The eyes that looked at me were full of greed. I told myself I was crazy for walking straight into such a den of impious thieves. But your mother maintained her magisterial air. That reassured me a little. She didn't turn back. She ignored the laughter from the women, the children reaching their hands out to her, the sharp looks from the warriors. She went straight to a small tree, under which the leaders of this pack of wolves seemed to be holding a *jemaa* [17].

As she approached, someone pointed a finger and said, "The women are on the other side."

Your mother responded, "I'm not a woman."

"You seem like one," retorted a man, around forty.

"I'm not a woman," your mother repeated, imperturbable, her head held high.

"A djinn then?"

"No, I was born of the crest that rises above the high mountain of Aoukar."

"You're from the Oulad Mahmoud!" said another man. He got up. His long, bushy hair hid a growing bald patch. His wrinkles were not those of old age. The open neck of his *boubou* showed a thick body slashed with black ridges. He was not large, but a power radiated from him. His smile was genuine, but there was no light in his eyes.

"Yes, I'm the daughter of the chief of all who live, settled or nomadic, in Aoukar. My mother is a direct descendent of Sharif Bou-bezoul."

"Those are two excellent reasons for us to welcome you and to request that you go to the women's tents, where we will offer you the hospitality your name merits."

---

17 Author's note: Tribal assembly.

"I'm not a woman, I told you. I'm a petitioner!"

"Your petition, noble lady, will be granted," said the man who seemed to be the chief. "But first you must accept our hospitality."

"I know the generosity of your heart is matched only by the strength of your arms. But I'm not able to stay for long."

"A day?"

"Not even an hour. I have a camp nearby."

"So what brings you here, noble woman?"

"My tents are just a few minutes' walk from here, two dunes away. I'm accompanied by my servant here, one of our family's *znaguis*, and my daughter, who is seriously ill and is taking a long rest cure. I chose this place so we could be near the Imraguens, allies of my tribe, who give me cod-liver oil, but also so we could be alone, in complete isolation for several weeks, to give my daughter a chance to heal. She can't tolerate noise, or certain smells, or meeting unknown people."

"So what do you want from us, noble woman?"

"For you not to compel me to find a new place to care for my daughter."

"Your will is granted, noble cousin. We've just put up our tents and the women and children are tired, but tomorrow we'll leave this place and seek other land."

"I never doubted the nobility of your hearts, but what woman of the sands could complain of having you as neighbours? What Saharan would not feel reassured to have you so close?"

"Noble woman, explain what it is you want!" growled another man.

"And we'll do it right away!" added a third.

"The Tekats will never waver in granting the wishes of a

woman in difficulty," the chief confirmed.

"All I want is for the peace and quiet my daughter needs to be respected," said your mother.

"You will be left in peace, noble woman," the chief replied. "No member of our clan will come near your tents, and we won't let anyone else invade your solitude either." '

Two months went by. They felt like centuries. The Tekats did not come near our camp. We saw them in the distance, disappearing as soon as we came out of our tents. Massouda left in the morning, often very early, and came back in the middle of the day to prepare a light lunch. The herdsman, terrorised by the presence of the Tekats, was even less in evidence than before. My mother seemed to take pleasure in our solitude. She lifted the tent flap and stared out into the distance, her face turned to the east. She hadn't the slightest interest in anything we said or did. She barely registered the baby's cries. Massouda confided her worries in me, 'Your mother is either going crazy, or she's plotting something. May Allah protect us from what we cannot know!'

One day my mother called us into her tent. I understood that the moment had come, that the water was now ready to gush out from the bed of the *wadi*. She turned to me. 'You deserve to die,' she told me. 'You have killed all hope of happiness in me forever, you have obliged me to bow my head, never again to raise my voice, you are a thunderbolt that struck me, when I had done no wrong. I've always been faithful to God and known my place. What did I do to deserve this, my only daughter giving birth to a nameless child? I wish I'd died the moment I heard about it. Why am I not dead? Perhaps it's a sign from God, my punishment for having closed my eyes: having to carry on living, bearing the unbearable. I am condemned, by your wrongdoing, to wander, soulless, in a world that will no longer speak to me. That's why I acted immediately to save what matters very little to me, our two lives, and what matters greatly to me, our family names. If your father knew, he would come back to cut both our throats, if my brother knew, he would banish us, and live the rest of his days in shame and sorrow. If the camp knew, the honour of our families would be tainted. I think I can prevent all of that, and even return to our frozen hearts a small semblance of life. The child will live, but faraway from us.'

I didn't know what to say. Her words seemed to float over me and disappear. I caught hold only of the phrase 'will live' and imagined immediately that my child would die. I burst into tears and started to beg, 'He mustn't die, he mustn't go, mother, it's me who should die, not him!' I grabbed the end of her veil and implored her, 'You can't do it, you mustn't!' Massouda held me and shouted repeatedly in my ear, 'Nothing bad is going to happen to your son, nothing bad!' I didn't hear her.

'Tell her, please, in the name of all the prophets and all the saints, of our Sheikh Tijane and all the other sheikhs, of her marabout ancestors and all her other ancestors too, that he mustn't die, he's my baby, I was wrong to have him, but he's my baby, he mustn't die. Crucify me, slit my throat in front of the *qibla*[18], as they would an animal, turn me into a herdswoman, or a slave, send me to live in the stench and

_____
18 Translator's note: the direction that should be faced when a Muslim prays.

97

debauchery of the cities of Satan, or amongst the diseased dung of a camel herd, make me the guardian of the Imraguen nets, a servant girl to the Tekats, but let him see the light of day, let him grow up, let me see him grow up, or let me not see him, but let him grow up at least!'

Massouda held me in her arms and cried with me. My mother stared at us, impassive. I saw the expression on her face through my tears, and it frightened me. It was one of unshakeable resolution: she'd banished tears and moved beyond doubt. I thought I saw a kind of madness behind her bulbous eyes, about to surge out and devour both of us. I stopped crying, shaken by the truth that had suddenly dawned on me: my mother was prepared to do anything, suicide, murder, anything, to get what she wanted. She was beyond all reason.

She resumed, as if speaking to herself, 'Massouda will take the child. He will live with her, he will want for nothing. I will provide everything they both need. She'll invent some story to explain him. We will return to the camp. If we stay here much longer, questions will start to be asked. People always think the worst. You will marry Memed. I think he'll keep quiet and accept you when he finds out you're not a virgin. I'll speak to him if necessary, but I'll make sure he keeps quiet. As for this ignominy, it never existed, my shame will never appear before anyone else's eyes. That is the price of the survival of all of us. Do you understand?'

Massouda and I remained silent. My mother did not expect a response, let alone an argument. A single breath would have brought a howl, a word and she would have rained all her anger down on us.

The life Mbarka led was an assault on my senses. Time moved at a strange tempo: moments seemed to spin past before I could take hold of them; days, nights and hours lost their rhythm; words, sensations, even fears, changed their meaning so I could no longer grasp them. It was a vibrant and fluid existence, though not one I could begin to understand. All I could do was watch from afar, contemplate the unknown, marvel at it, sometimes laugh, sometimes make a tentative approach, listen then move away, terrorised. Even if I'd had the courage to examine my deep, secret desires, it wouldn't have been possible: I'd drawn a line under that aspect of life. I had no wish to antagonise good spirits or entertain false people, and my own error and flight meant I was in no position to pass judgement on anyone. I was so ignorant and backward compared to Mbarka's friends that I didn't dare open my mouth in their presence. They would have had a good laugh at the silly little Bedouin.

Mbarka had many friends. Men and women came and went, laughing, shouting, playing music, dancing. They never seemed to rest; they would still be there long after nightfall, shrieking with laughter. Sometimes I heard heavy breathing in the room adjoining mine, then it would stop, those who'd been making love would go back to join the group in the courtyard, another couple would replace them, and the breathing would start again. It sickened me sometimes, but I told myself I was Mbarka's guest. I had to keep quiet and accept the life she led; she was making up for hours, days and nights of suffering, drying her tears by drinking from the full goatskin of life, so her sadness could never return. I knew, of course, that all the activity was a form of deception, a mask used to hide from time, and deep down, I felt sorry for my friend: every night she plunged into stormy seas, fishing for the golden pearls of oblivion. The years passed and the miracle catch never appeared.

I watched the whole circus from afar, because from the very first day Mbarka had placed a barrier between it and me, 'None of this is for you. You're different, you're from a good family, you're still very young, you have another kind of future ahead of you, a real one. And you're my sister. I forbid you from interacting with this dark world of mine. You'll stay clean. Whenever they're here, keep yourself apart. Stay in this room, which is yours alone. Even I feel tired of it all sometimes, but you know how it is. You can't choose your fate.'

So I became a passive observer at the parties where Mbarka danced.

Amongst Mbarka's friends, Hama visited the most. He had gradually become my friend too. I'd forgotten the repulsion I'd first felt at his effeminate gestures, the way he waved his slender arms around, the wiggle of his hips, his singsong voice. He often left Mbarka and her entourage and came to keep me company. This disturbed me at first. I wanted to be alone, to brood undisturbed about the little soul I'd lost, to try to work out how to find him, and to feed myself every day with new reasons to hate my tribe and my clan. Hama disturbed my private conversations with my hate. Mbarka often dragged him away too, shouting, 'Hama, come out of there, leave my sister alone, she's not part of your world, you degenerate!' He would leave immediately, with a gracious little wave of his hand.

Hama, I soon discovered, was a treasure. He knew the whole city, the whole country in fact. He could recite numerous poems. He told me stories of true loves and dubious relations. He was very funny. He guided me gently towards some understanding of the failings and the falsehoods of people. He had a beautiful voice and was a virtuoso on the tom-tom, which he could beat with one hand, two hands, one foot, two feet, all while dancing. He gave me a demonstration that left me flabbergasted.

His curious eyes alighted one day on the drum. I'd hidden it behind a large cushion, wrapped in a thick veil. He gave an admiring whistle and reached for it. I jumped up and pushed him away. He was astonished. I didn't understand the violence of my reaction myself. It was crazy, but in that moment I'd been ready to kill to prevent Hama from touching the drum. It was as if I was protecting the Black Stone[19], or some other sacred thing, as if by allowing Hama's hand to touch the drum I would be committing sacrilege. Hama laughed to hide his surprise, and said, 'She's hiding Ali Baba's treasure under her clothes!'

Mbarka rebuked him. 'How dare you touch my sister's things? I've told you she's different. I want her to stay different.

---

19 Translator's note: a sacred rock, part of the Grand Mosque in Mecca.

I forbid you from going near her ever again!'

I was a little ashamed of my impulse and spent all night reflecting on my action. Was I still in thrall to their myths, still capable of blind adoration of their icon? Were their values still so ingrained in me, the same values that had oppressed me, that had led to the theft of the fruit of my womb and threatened my life? Was I still a prisoner to my mother and uncle, to the father who had so easily abandoned me? I was tempted to destroy the drum, to break it into a thousand pieces, to burn it and call Hama and Mbarka so we could all dance around it. But I told myself that the spoils of war should not be destroyed, they should continue to exist, so the insult could continue. The tribe must never forget that I, the weak young girl, the sinner, the lost daughter, the bad seed, held the symbol of their pride in my hands, the mass of leather and wood they'd made their sacred totem, though they liked to consider themselves Muslims. I repeated to myself that I held in my hands their *Ellatt*, their *Ouza*,[20] their ancient idol, and that I would bestow on the lowly, marginal Hama the right to touch that old relic, to spit, if he wanted to, on that object of false worship. From the next day on, I'd let him use the drum to make sounds that were more harmonious than their chants of war and ruin. I'd keep hold of my hostage; it was the price they had to pay for my suffering and my flight. When I found my child, I would offer it to him as his very first toy. When he broke it with his un-coordinated little hands, or stamped on it with his clumsy feet, I'd be happy. I'd know their drum was dead, their traces had been erased.

I explained everything to Hama. He refused to touch the

---

20 Author's note: *Ellat* and *Ouza*, idols of pre-Islamic Arabia.

drum after that. He was moved by my story and prayed to the heavens to help me find my son. Mbarka mocked his demonstration of faith, 'Don't spoil everything, Hama! How could the good Lord be deaf to the appeals of my friend but respond to a reprobate like you?'

It was old Fatmouha who kept me company most of the time. She left her shack every morning to come to Mbarka's house. There she fried *beignets* that she sold in the town, did the cleaning, sometimes cooked a meal. I tried to help her, but I had trouble keeping up with the old lady's frenetic pace. Mbarka's former protector had become her protégé. She worshipped Mbarka, though when they were together she often admonished her, 'What is this life you're leading, my girl? You're courting the devil, forgetting God and the prophet, forgetting the final judgement!' Mbarka let the insults wash over her. Sometimes she maliciously reminded Fatmouha of her own mis-spent youth. The old lady alluded to it herself on occasion, 'I wasn't always old and hunched, little one. I was young once, I broke plenty of hearts. Not wicked, bloodless hearts like the ones that come through this door, but real hearts, men from good families, with spirit and energy, and also sometimes a nice watch or a pretty snuffbox. Real men, not like the flashy types you see today, who don't have a clue about the world.'

When Fatmouha was in a good mood, she'd throw down her cowrie shells and become a fortune teller. She always gave me the rosiest of futures, 'There's that shell again, look: a faraway woman who's ashamed because you've beaten her, because the evil she wished for you has fled; and that one, the sign for a great joy that inhabits the whole body, and that one, that's real love, little one, a paradise that awaits you.' She made me take the shells of good fortune in my hands and bring them to my lips. Fatmouha's cowries only ever presaged the good things: love, marriage, joy and health.

Mbarka took on the task of re-creating me. I could not remain poor, suffering Rayhana, the Bedouin with the uncertain smile, the permanently bewildered look, the end of her veil trailing in the dirt. It was time for me to dive into the city, to dress as the city people did, to draw an invisible line around myself, as they did, to stop interacting spontaneously with others. 'The city,' Mbarka told me, 'has two types of people. The real citizens were born here, have roots here, feel at home here. They belong to the stones and the streets and know how to mould themselves to them. Those people have the city's habits. They speak its language. They can be condescending, contemptuous even. The other type is those who still hold their desert or their oasis in their hearts. If you want to be invisible, and stop your tribe from finding you, you have to learn to behave like the real citizens.' My veil, she said, had to be bright, cheerful, clean, and not drag on the ground. I had to walk around smiling in a careless, sometimes mocking, way. I had to show my legs, and occasionally my hair. Most of all, I should never be linked to the dregs of the city.

I couldn't inhabit the character she'd created for me. I didn't know how to walk like the city people, to express myself the way they did, using words that seemed to me to be without sense, or power, or intelligence. City people said what they wanted to say and no more. There was no musicality or emotion in their words. The attitudes Mbarka instructed me to imitate didn't speak to me: I had no desire to be like these people.

I tried, but neither my walk nor my bearing, neither my curious glances nor my language, could fail to betray me. I was clearly from elsewhere: from the lands that were white with sand and black with fury.

I didn't want to waste time with showy actions or words. I wanted to find my baby. Mbarka and her friends set to work helping me.

Mbarka spent the mornings asleep. When she got up, she would go out and wander through the town for hours in search of my child. When she returned, she barely had time to give me a quick report of her day and offer a few thoughts before she had to make herself beautiful in preparation for another night of music, socialising, laughter and love.

Mbarka had a raw terror of the people of our tribe. She spoke as if they might appear at any moment, filling the air with their murderous cries. I was forbidden from going to the market (too dangerous), from visiting my former hosts (too dangerous), from going to places where there were parties (too dangerous). The words 'too dangerous' were forever on Mbarka's lips. She had an instinctive and superstitious fear of the drum: she wouldn't touch it, or even glance in its direction. Whenever I took it out of the cloth it was wrapped in, Mbarka would close her eyes. She said she could hear the plundering, the fury, the cries of war. She saw her mother, crushed by slavery and poverty. I hit the *tobol* hard, so the rumble from its weather-beaten skin could penetrate her hearing. I wanted that heavy, shapeless sound to be something real and present, so she could liberate herself from it.

During those early days at Mbarka's, I didn't leave the house. I waited inside for Mbarka and her friends to bring news. Khattri told his customers invented stories of children from faraway, lost in unusual circumstances, to try to encourage them to talk. He told me people often chatted to him, but they offered no leads. Hama did as much as he could. He was close to many businesspeople in the town, and he spoke to them about a cousin who'd lost her child. Whenever he was invited to a wedding, he asked around. Mbarka walked the length of the city every day, even crossing the *wadi* and going as far as Eddebay. Sometimes she walked around the vast cement and stone house of the great marabout Ely Cheikh, where crowds of people gathered, from the deserts and the towns. She found nothing.

My heart nearly stopped one day when Hama told me he'd heard about a family who had adopted several abandoned children. We planned to visit them the next morning. I didn't sleep that night. We used no subterfuge to enter their house, we simply arrived as they were opening the front door to welcome the fresh morning air into their humble home. Three shabby, bare-bottomed little things sat facing the wall. They were struggling to write wobbly letters of the alphabet. I was going to say something to make them turn round, but there was no need; I knew straightaway none of them were mine. I made a sign to Mbarka and we retraced our steps. My heart ached and I couldn't stop the tears from flowing.

While I waited for news, I helped Fatmouha to sell her *beignets* outside schools. She would begin preparing them in Mbarka's courtyard from dawn, filling the whole house with frying smells. I learned to knead and shape the dough of flour and egg and to cook the spicy sauce, a mixture of onion, garlic, tomato puree, pepper and salt, which I could never taste without coughing. Sometimes I went to stand at the school gates with Fatmouha, despite her protests and those of Mbarka. We got there at break time and I watched the children laughing and playing. I tried to talk to them, to stroke their heads, but they frowned at me and rarely replied. Fatmouha scolded me whenever I offered a free *beignet* to children who gave me an imploring look, though I'd seen her do the same herself.

In the evenings, I began to sneak away from Mbarka's house and go into the centre of town. I sat on the low wall of the '*poinronh*' and watched people and cars passing. The drivers stopped outside shops and called out to the sellers, who brought their purchases straight to their cars. Women wearing make-up and beautiful jewellery sat next to the drivers. I envied them. I day-dreamed about being one of them, sitting there and demanding whatever I wanted. Being beautiful in town meant ordering men around with just a murmur, a gesture, a blink of the eye. Sometimes one of the drivers would signal to me. I would swiftly turn my head away. Young couples sat in the middle of the circle chatting. The girls wore clean, brightly coloured veils, strands of hair escaping at the edges. Exotic perfumes floated around them. The boys wore blue or white *boubous* with short shirts. They spoke loudly, as if to make the space itself and all the people in it aware of their presence. Their raucous laughter and their flirting turned my stomach. It was a happiness that seemed forced, that hid itself in cryptic words and phrases. It pretended to be coy, but it was destructive; it had destroyed me. Sometimes I wanted to shout to the girls, 'Don't believe it! Don't be fooled by poetic words, or by the illusions our men try to sell you!' But the girls threw hostile glances in my direction, as if I was intruding on their experience. I wanted to retort, 'Do you think I'm not good enough to sit beside you? Look at me! Am I not beautiful enough for you?'

One day I met the twins. They were coming out of a shop with some other girls, all talking at once, their laughter filling the air. I was about to run in the opposite direction when Selma saw me. She detached herself from the group and came towards me.

'You're here! We wondered what had happened to you! Mother said you found the sister you were looking for. You could've come back to see us though!'

Jemila joined us. She embraced me. 'Our little lost Bedouin who was looking for a Mbarka! She's put on some weight. Look how beautiful she's got!'

I wasn't sure how to reply. I wasn't unhappy to see them. I babbled my gratitude, 'You were good to me, and your mother is the best woman in the world.' One of their friends came over and pointed at me, saying 'I've seen her before! She lives with Mbarka, a freed slave with a bad reputation.' The twins started to lecture me. I distanced myself, mumbling, 'No, Mbarka is my sister. I love her very much.' Then I ran from them.

Mbarka decided I needed an identity card. She had a friend in the police who would help us for nothing. 'We should take advantage of it while we can,' she told me. 'It might be much harder and more expensive in the future.' She took me to a photographer who made me adopt an idiotic expression. 'You only have to do it once, then you can use it for everything,'

Mbarka reassured me. The next day, we went to the police station. The policeman was waiting for us. He placed my hand on the black ink and called on witnesses I'd never met before to attest that I was indeed Rayhana, from the tribe of the Smacides, born in Terwen, a *wadi* I'd never seen in my life. The document was given to me immediately. I was surprised to feel nothing when I held this passport to civilisation in my hands. Why was a document required to know who someone was? Why not just use tribe, clan, family? Where I came from, everyone was part of a tribe and all the tribes spoke to and understood each other. Everyone knew their own people well, our camels had our brands on them, and it would never occur to anyone to hide their roots. Apart for me, today.

I hadn't come to town to get papers, or to see a lifeless version of my face be swallowed up by a machine. I'd come to find Marvoud.

The clamour of impatience was getting louder inside me. There was a permanent dry taste of weariness in my mouth. I wanted to sleep, but sleep wouldn't come. I felt heavy, I had headaches, I hated the universe. I longed for solitude, but people and things were everywhere, and I was always on the outside, watching. I couldn't stand the constant noise; there seemed to be shouting all around me, even when the city and its people were asleep.

One evening I stormed into the living room where Mbarka and her friends were listening to music and dancing. I aimed a kick at their screeching sound machine, and shouted, 'You're making me ill with your disgusting behaviour, you're crushing my spirit with your constant partying! You never think about anything important! Don't you even see me? Look at me, you bunch of slobs! I'm nothing. I'm the emptiness that wanders the streets in search of peace, rest, existence, life. Has anyone ever stolen a life from you, stolen the first steps of your child, its first smiles, its uncoordinated movements, its first word, "Mama!" Have you ever walked amongst strangers, been present without anyone ever looking at you? You're all rotten to the core!' As soon as I'd spoken, I fell to the floor, drained, and blacked out.

Mbarka and Fatmouha blamed my strange behaviour on djinns. They said malevolent forces had taken advantage of my weakness, innocence and solitude to possess me. They took me to see a marabout. He was not just any marabout, but the best in town, and the most expensive, consulted by rich ladies who wanted to know how to hold on to their husbands, and state officials who dreamed of promotion. Fatmouha explained that the djinns were afraid of this marabout, who knew how to burn them using Quranic verses. She described miracles he'd performed, women who'd never been able to conceive falling pregnant thanks to him, men cured of illnesses that doctors had no medicine for. She told me the famous story of the two men fighting over the same camel. The great marabout had made the camel speak. 'Which of these men do you belong to, creature of God?' he'd asked it, and the camel had pronounced the name of its master.

The marabout's house was on the other side of town. We sat on the ground in a dark, dirty courtyard, waiting, surrounded by many women, most of whom had their faces veiled. Mbarka whispered in my ear, 'They don't want to be recognised because they're trying to bewitch their husbands, or steal other women's husbands, or capture the hearts of rich, powerful men. They're sneering at us because we're not from their world.' Fatmouha said nothing, just mumbled prayers. We were soon called through into a dimly-lit room furnished with a large mat and many cushions. The marabout sat on a throne at the back. He wore a large turban. I couldn't make out much of his face, but the silhouette of his nose on the wall looked immeasurably long, and his eyes looked like those of a satyr. A shiver ran through me. He asked us to sit down. It was Fatmouha who took the seat beside him and spoke for us.

'My daughter here,' she said in a hesitant voice, 'has lost her child, he was stolen from her. May your powers assist her in finding the apple of her eye. She also suffers from headaches, she doesn't sleep, sometimes she has hysterical fits. We await your benediction and that of your ancestors.'

The marabout closed his eyes and said some inaudible words, then suddenly pointed his finger at me.

'Do you believe in me?'

'Yes, of course,' I stammered, terrified.

'Do you believe in my family?'

'Yes, of course,' I repeated.

'The voices are telling me your health will improve and you will find your son. Carry the talisman I'm going to give you and the djinns will stay away. Drink the water I give you and your wishes will be granted, but don't forget me, your marabout, or worse ills will rain down on you, and no one will be able to help you then.'

He gave Fatmouha an amulet and a handful of sand, which she took with care in cupped hands. He said, 'She should throw a little of this sand into a glass of water and sprinkle it on herself, and she should never be without the talisman. Come back to me when she's regained her health and found her son.'

Fatmouha gave a long speech about the virtues of the marabout's Cherifean lineage, the miracles enacted by his forefathers, their mastery of the Quran and the Hadith, the special place they would occupy next to the prophet on the day of judgement. The marabout merely nodded in response. Mbarka opened her bag, took out several notes and laid them on the mat. The marabout made no movement towards the money. We left the room in silence.

As we were leaving, Mbarka suddenly grabbed my hand and pulled me with her into a run. Behind us, Fatmouha was shouting, 'Where are you going? What djinn is riding you?' Mbarka dragged me along at a frenetic pace, our hair streaming in the wind. I understood nothing, but I sensed danger, and I ran as fast as my legs could carry me. Mbarka was faster. Occasionally she looked back and urged me to speed up. She held her shoes in her hand; I had cast mine aside. Pebbles and gravel chafed my feet, but I was too frightened to feel pain. I felt as if I was flying. People turned and giggled as we passed them, men opened their arms, laughing, as if to catch us, women murmured, 'They're crazy!' We registered nothing, we just ran. Finally, at the door of Mbarka's house, we stopped, bent double, panting. That was when I realised I no longer had my shoes, that my feet were bleeding a little and that Mbarka was shivering with fear. Her dress was torn, her hair tousled, she was sweating and her whole body trembled. Her face was anxious. She was close to tears.

'Did you see?' she asked. 'Did you see what I saw?'

'I didn't see anything, I just ran with you.'

'They were there.'

'Who?'

'You didn't see them? Their faces were half-hidden by black turbans, but I recognised them all right.'

'Who?'

'Men from the camp!'

I felt astonished rather than afraid. I thought I'd covered my traces and was now definitively out of reach, because I'd crossed the sea of sand and entered another world, a distant continent. I couldn't imagine any passage between the two sides.

'I don't think they saw us,' Mbarka added. 'They weren't looking our way.'

She was trying to reassure me, but I couldn't respond. The words were stuck in my throat.

'They're probably not looking for you, they'd just come to see the marabout,' she said.

We were joined by an out of breath Fatmouha. 'Do you want rid of me, girls? Are you trying to give me a heart attack?'

Mbarka locked the house door that evening and let only Hama in. She was in shock, frightened for both of us. Hama tried to calm her down, but she brushed away his soothing hand.

'You don't know them, Hama! They're monsters, they're capable of anything. They might embrace you one minute and murder you the next, recite a poem while slitting your throat and think themselves anointed by the good Lord for doing so, strangle you half to death while drowning you in pious proclamations. They'd stop at nothing to see us tied up and thrown to the wolves on their ancestral land. They're monsters, Hama, and I'll protect my sister from them if I die doing it!'

Mbarka, only half-clothed, paced around the small room like a crazy person. I was stunned into silence. Before me I saw dense mists and through them I saw Marvoud, calling out to me.

Finally I roused myself from my stupor and said 'Mbarka, it's only me they want. I'm the one who stole their idol and trampled on their stupid pride. I don't want you to have to pay for what I did. I'll leave. I'll be able to evade them.'

'You're wrong, sister! We're bound together for life; we're like one being!'

Both of us started to cry. It took Hama a long time to soothe us. He made a strange proposition:

'I've told you before, Mbarka, Atar isn't a city you can hide in for long. It's really just a big oasis, open to the four winds: people meet here, know each other, news travels, everyone lives in close proximity. You two think you're in the city because you only know the desert. But those Bedouins are smarter than you. To make the child disappear they'll have sent him to the real city: a modern city, one swarming with life, like a whole faceless country, full of everything you can imagine. They will have taken him to Nouakchott. That's where Rayhana must go too, to escape her people and find her child.'

'If she goes, I go!' said Mbarka.

'You'd be no use to her there,' he said. 'You don't know the place, it's huge and anarchic and you'd just be another thing for her to worry about. It's me who should go, just until she's settled in with my older sister, a good woman who'll look after her. I'll come back soon, because it won't take them long to find out where you are, and they'll know you're my friend. They won't do us any harm; it would be shameful in their eyes to have dealings with freed slaves like us, leading sinful lives, they wouldn't taint their hands by touching us, but they will watch us, follow us everywhere, we won't notice a thing but they'll always be one step behind us. These are people who hunt gazelles, remember. They'll wait a long time for a sign, a clue to lead them to Rayhana. As soon as they see her or discover where she's hiding, they'll swoop on her like hawks, and skin her alive, just to erase their shame, or, "Wash the water from their faces," as they'd say.'

'They're monsters, I know! That's why I won't let her face them alone. I'll stay with her.'

'She won't be alone. My sister and my nephew will be with her. My sister's a rich businesswoman. She's also kind and thoughtful. My nephew is twenty, he's a good boy, open and brave, he studies hard and he knows Nouakchott like the back of his hand. He'll help her look for her child. Rayhana is intelligent and strong, Mbarka. She knows how to survive. Let her follow her path. She won't have to hide the way she did here: Nouakchott is a horribly huge place, it's a place where even twins would lose each other. Let her go, Mbarka. She'll want for nothing. We'll take the jewellery and I'll sell it for her there, I'll get a good price. When everything's calmed down, she'll come back here, hopefully with her child in her arms.'

Mbarka rejected the suggestion at first. What an idea, she scoffed, to send an ignorant Bedouin to a city filled with all that is vulgar and superficial, a place with no sky, where people not only rub shoulders with each other but sometimes knife each other, a city that belongs to another world, a world devoid of love or honour! But I could see that Hama was right, that I would have to go to this place to find my child.

We practically galloped back to the camp, my mother allowing no respite to the camels or their drivers, so eager was she to get home. I hid under my palanquin, shaken by the jolting, and covered my face to hide my tears. I'd left a little part of me behind, and Massouda too; I was separated from the sweet young fruit of my sin and from the old Imraguen who'd sheltered me with her compassion. I was lost to all joy, and I was going to have to lie if I was to continue living, under a sky that had disappeared. I did at least feel less anxious about my child's future: I knew Massouda would take good care of him, would make sure he grew up healthy and strong. I hoped that, despite my mother's instructions, she wouldn't keep my memory from him forever. One day, perhaps... but I closed my eyes to the rays of hope that threatened to blind me. The path I would now have to walk was a rocky one, but I had no choice but to follow it.

As we prepared to mount our camels, my mother was still whispering in Massouda's ear, 'That child must be seen by everyone to be yours, you must see him that way yourself. He no longer has a mother, the name of my unworthy daughter must never be pronounced in his presence, not even when he grows up, nor my name, nor that of our family. That connection is a tree with no trunk or roots; it is dead to both of us and it should not exist for anyone else either. I will send enough money for you to live well, but I insist on absolute secrecy.' Massouda agreed with a grave nod of the head. I knew she was pleased with the outcome, because it liberated me and saved the child's life, but also because she herself had become attached to my son.

The excitement at our arrival caught me unawares. Women ululated, men placed their hands on their hearts to express their joy, a griot plucked his *tidinitt*[21] and sang the praises of my mother and her ancestors, the blacksmiths and the slaves all applauded and gently nodded their heads. The tribal *tobol* even sounded. Our camels were taken by their reins and made to kneel so our things could be quickly unloaded. A crowd of people surrounded us, all asking the same questions, 'Are you well? Did the Imraguens take good care of you? You weren't too bothered by the fishy smells? How did you both get so beautiful?' Behind my mother's terse smile I recognised a deep wound, but also a secret pride, that of being seen to be celebrated on her return to her people, a testimony to her importance in the tribe. The whole camp had been waiting for us. Only the chief and the older noblemen were absent; they didn't mix with the young people, the women and the rank and file. They were waiting until the excitement had passed, then they'd come one at a time to greet my mother. I was surrounded by girls of my own age, who exclaimed enthusiastically and cried with joy as they embraced me. People kept telling me how beautiful I looked. My friends' glances were part admiring, part envious. They whispered in

---

21 Author's note: Musical instrument.

my ear, 'You'll make an excellent wife.' I'd had no idea I was pretty; I didn't know I'd soaked up the sun, put on weight, got new colour in my cheeks.

Our tent that night was the scene of endless bowing and scraping; you'd have thought we'd left the camp a century ago. My mother began to lose her voice, my muscles ached from jumping up all the time to embrace the women of our tribe.

Late at night, when we finally found ourselves alone, and despite our extreme fatigue, our pains, the shadows under our eyes, the yawns I could no longer suppress, my mother began to talk to me, in a low voice so that no one would overhear, 'Now we're back with our people, at home, surrounded by our tribe and our clan, this month of suffering must be buried, erased definitively from our minds and our memories. No one must learn of what we went through, not one single soul. Our tongues must never speak of it. You know that the ember you ignited in my heart and in my guts will continue to burn, and will cause me eternal suffering, but we must be silent and forget. We must let time pass. Perhaps one day our burden will feel less heavy.' I didn't answer her. I wrapped myself up tightly in a big *burnous* and cried all night.

I dreamed I was returning to the camp with my child in my arms. No one was waiting for us. We walked alone, under the moonlight, through a silent desert. The tent flaps stirred but no sound came from the flimsy dwellings that trembled in the wind. Even the night birds were hiding. I kept moving forward, my stride resolute, my little love in my arms, shouting, 'Here it is – my sin, my pain! I want all of you to bless it, to forget shame and remember life! I want to see you welcome this little person just as you welcomed my mother. He's mine, and hers too. He belongs to all of you. I want to see him running between your tents, and I want no one ever to point a finger at him!' No voice responded. Suddenly an enormous jackal, as big as a lion, ran out of the chief's tent, jaws bared. It reared up on its hind legs and howled. I could hear laughter in the distance, then I noticed the whole camp was watching, encouraging the beast. I stopped, laid the baby down, seized a spear and screamed at the top of my voice, 'No one will devour my heart!' I woke with a start, just as the jackal was preparing to leap at me.

For the first few days after we got back I didn't leave the tent. My mother continued to receive visits from neighbours and relatives from other camps. They asked after my health, touched my head, lifted up my eyelids, thanked God for having cured me. Oumou was widely praised for having accurately diagnosed my illness and sent me to the Imraguens. Of course they all declared me pretty and advised my mother I should marry, 'Such beauty demands a good husband. Every man in the Sahara dreams of such a well-born nymph.' My mother always replied that she had her choice of suitors, that many offers had been made, but first I had to regain my health and then my father had to give his consent; my father who had not been seen at the camp since his departure and about whom no one knew a thing. Everyone knew that in fact it had all already been decided.

Nothing had changed at the camp except the teacher, who'd been sent back to town. The whole camp had turned against him. He'd committed the unpardonable sin of publicly

120

contradicting the chief. The chief had called the nomadic members of our tribe across the whole region to come to our camp for the census, to try to convince the government to set up one or two voting booths amongst our tents. That way, he explained, the importance of our tribe would be affirmed, and we could also contribute to the victory of the current administration's candidate, and so gain favour with them. Emissaries and gifts had been sent to all the clan chiefs, and the tribal drum had sounded every night.

The teacher disagreed with the initiative. After the Friday prayer at the mosque he announced that he considered it an impious act: it was deceitful and treasonous to seek to mobilise a mass of ignorant Bedouins to vote for a corrupt administration. His reaction offended the men of the camp, 'Who does he think he is, this city man who seems to have discovered the Good Lord only yesterday, interfering when he isn't even part of our tribe, or any of our clans? Doesn't he know that this modern politics, these parties and elections, are the mere whims of people with nothing else to do? They're not important, like rain, or wells, or camels! Doesn't he know that only the government, whichever one it is, can dig our wells for us, deliver our provisions and the fodder for our animals? How dare he call us ignorant! He doesn't even know how to read an animal's tracks, get a camel to kneel, milk a goat or find his way in the dark in our vast Sahara. Is there anyone more ignorant than someone who can't find their way?' They reminded themselves of his tactlessness, the way he'd insulted the Sufi sheiks, the prayers he'd tried to force even the slaves to understand, his constant intrusions into everyone's lives. The herdsmen added their opinion too: his red beard and booming voice frightened their camels.

Memed was suggested as a temporary replacement for the teacher, until the administration sent a new one. The chief agreed and everyone praised Memed, such a good son of the tribe, someone who'd been to town, who knew the world and even foreign languages, who'd never allowed his head to be turned by the bright mirages of the villainous city, who'd always respected his people and their traditions.

The camp had forgotten about the *Nçaras*. The land they'd occupied was bare and black. The Bedouins were convinced that djinns prowled around the former camp at night, that on the eve of Good Friday they met to dance a wild dance around the accumulated waste. Everyone avoided the place. Herdsmen called to nomads they saw in the distance who seemed to be passing too close to it, warning them that if their animals went there, they would come back with cracked feet, their women would lose their fertility, their men their virility. The former camp was marked with a black cross in people's minds.

I looked at my camp with new eyes. Life seemed to drift along meaninglessly. There was a kind of languid vacancy in the air and on people's faces. I tried to respond to the demands of my daily life: receiving visitors, listening to pointless gossip. I always had my responses ready: 'Welcome! Well said! Wonderful! That's very true! May Allah bless you! May the rain follow in your footsteps!' I served them milk and prepared tea. I behaved like a virtuous and well brought up young woman.

My friends tried to drag me along to their evening gatherings on top of the highest dune. I came up with a thousand other things I had to do, but I resolved that one day I'd explain to them that I was now lost to their childish games and innocent flirtations. At night, I sometimes pressed my hands over my ears to stop the sound of their singing and their ringing laugher from opening old wounds.

Memed sacrificed a camel in our honour and came to see us. He didn't say a word to me, but spoke for a long time with my mother. I knew it was about me, but I only caught a few snatches. My old resolution returned: I would belong to no one. I was lost to myself, so how could I give myself to anyone else? Memed could chase me all he liked, I would never belong to him. My destiny was mapped out: no one could be allowed to see my stain. I would kill myself if necessary, stick a dagger in my throat before compromising. I would refuse with all my strength to give myself over, and then maybe, one day, if I survived...

Memed's mother came to see us too. She was the polar opposite of her son: a woman formed entirely of curves, with a pleasant face, who talked non-stop, laughed at nothing at all and had an opinion on everything. After speaking for some time with my mother, she called me to her side, pushed her elbow into my right leg and, uncovering her head, demanded I de-louse her. It was an old game played by future mother-in-laws to test the manners and patience of the potential spouse. I gritted my teeth and played along.

Things moved forward more quickly than I'd expected. One afternoon a whole crowd of women appeared at our tent and the griots began to sing and play their instruments. My mother simply whispered in my ear as she passed me on her way to welcome the guests, 'You're marrying Memed.' I was struck

123

dumb. My friends rushed to congratulate me. They pulled my veil, jostled me, those who weren't married yet pressed their foreheads to mine so I could bring them good luck. I was expected to hide my face and show no pleasure, which wasn't difficult. Soon, I was told, the men and the older women would go to my uncle to seal the marriage contract. Its clauses would be those demanded by our religion and our customs. I could already hear the stern voice of my mother reciting the old rules in a monotone, rules that were not always respected, 'He should not be linked to any woman, he should not take another for as long as he does not renounce my daughter, he should respect her and her family, he should not hit her, or say hurtful words to her, he should not insult her tribe or her clan, he should support her as much as his means allow, and the day he breaches any of these conditions, she will consider herself free and de facto divorced.' I saw my uncle nodding his head, Memed's father vowing that his son would respect the conditions, saying they were honoured by the union.

Seven ululations announced the marriage, and the tribal drum sounded seven times to proclaim the event. There was commotion all over the camp. I was taken into a tent to have my hair braided and my hands and feet tinted with henna in preparation for the ceremony. Everything had happened so fast. I was appalled. I was surrounded by shouting and frenetic activity, gripped by a thousand different pains, pulled between the tribal artisans, one working on my left hand, another on my right, one loosening my hair, another uncovering my feet. My face was veiled, and on no account was I permitted to speak; I had to be mute and crying. I couldn't laugh, or say the name of my husband or his family. It was tradition: virgins were meant to understand nothing, to submit passively to whatever happened to them. Women came in and out of the tent, chatting, sometimes dancing in rings around me. My friends acted as my guardians, surrounding me, pressing so close I felt suffocated. Old women knelt in front of me, lifted the veil from my face, uncovered my chest and enthused, '*Machallah*, may God preserve these fine features, this well-shaped body, these breasts that will feed beautiful children!' I was close to fainting. No one paid any attention to my suffering.

In the evening, Memed came, accompanied by the young men of the camp. He wore a white *boubou* and had a black turban around his neck. His face glowed with happiness. The women began to shout, dance and applaud. They congratulated and mocked him at the same time, calling him, 'Monkey!' and 'Billy goat!' That was tradition too: the bride was supposed to be beautiful and the groom ugly. They put him next to me and he draped his arm around my neck. I was shocked by this easy familiarity from someone usually so timid, then I remembered that in the last hour he had become my husband. I belonged to him now. A freed slave snatched a bracelet from my arm and started to dance around singing, displaying it to everyone, 'I stole the bride's bracelet, look at what I took from the bride!' A friend of Memed's gave her a bundle of notes and she lifted them high and waved them around like a trophy, shouting more loudly than ever, 'We stole the bride's bracelet, this is the ransom for the bride's bracelet!' The tents heaved with people, their singing and laughter rising up to the sky. Memed's friends made a circle around us, while my friends stuck to my side. After much forceful jostling, the men allowed just a few girls to stay with me. It was an old fight: the friends of the bride were meant to use all the tricks and wiles they could to keep her away from the groom, so the groom could demonstrate his love by fighting to get her back. The groom and his friends had to stay vigilant and not let the new bride fall into the hands of her friends. They were supposed to protect her using any means necessary, even violence. In the midst of all this hubbub, the bride had to remain unprotesting and unresisting; she represented innocence and ignorance, led one way then the other, a fragile object of love buffeted between the winds.

Tents had been erected at the edge of the camp. Griots had come from faraway. I heard the noise of the party and marvelled that it was for me, that they had all been planning and organising it for some time, without breathing a word. I was a puppet, an inert thing with no will of my own. My uncle, my mother, Memed and his family, had arranged it without talking to me, except to indicate that a new life was beginning for me, with new codes, new lies, endless new false nods and smiles.

They didn't know I was spoiled for everything forever, that life had already dropped its wreath at my feet and departed, that I had bid farewell to all ambitions for a happy home, and that Memed would never find in me the wife he had the right to expect.

The henna session lasted for several hours. My whole body was stiff and aching, but the women of the camp were ecstatic at the result. I was decorated with figures, ellipses, smooth lines that met and then separated, resembling birds' claws, or open mouths, or flowing water. My hands and feet showed a work of art that was doomed to fade and disappear. My hair was equally superb, piled high and glittering with all the jewels my mother had been able to borrow or buy. My locks were long, and the whole thing made my head heavy. Gems of every colour danced in front of my face and hung down over my chest.

At the party my head felt even heavier because of Memed's arm around my neck. He murmured irritating pledges of love in my ear throughout the evening. All the young people in the camp paraded past us noisily. The tents were arranged in a semi-circle in a large space. The crowd of people had come from all over; even, they told me, from the towns. The air was full of the sounds of the *ardine* and the *tidinitt*[22]. As we approached, cries burst forth, people ran to meet us, and in the midst of the crush, griots, their hands to their ears, sang a hymn in our honour. A small platform had been constructed for us and covered with red Moroccan rugs and soft cushions. As soon as we sat down on it, the griots began to intone their *t'heydines*, poems composed in honour of our tribe. The intoxication began: the women danced, the young men uncovered their heads, puffed out their chests and threw down everything they had on them: banknotes, watches, turbans, their *boubous*, locks of their hair... the *t'heydine* brings out the craziness in people. It glorifies the tribe's history, reminds us of our ancient values and the heroism of the past. It goes to people's heads. I'd never liked the *t'heydine*. Now it represented my uncle, my mother, the theft of my secret little soul, his handing over to Massouda, and I hated it more fiercely than ever. My uncle, the chief, was extolled, and there were songs dedicated to Memed's father, who was surprised and flattered, and to Memed's uncle, the

---

22 Author's note: Musical instruments played only by women.

richest man in the tribe, so generous, who, 'Gives and gives and forgets he has given.' None of it seemed relevant to me. I was dead, and no one even noticed.

A special newly-wed tent was erected for the two of us. It was woven from white wool and flooded with incense and myrrh. A horde of joyful people accompanied us to it. Memed enclosed me in his arms. The jeers about the ugly husband and the compliments to the bride accompanied the music of the griots. Memed's friends stayed with us, while my companions tried thousands of ruses to steal me away, in full view of the crowd; they said we had to go and re-do our make-up, that my hair needed adjusting, which couldn't be done in front of the men, that I needed air, that I would faint if I didn't get some. Memed's friends kept a close watch and thwarted all attempts at escape.

I was bounced between the machinations of my friends and the protective ardour of Memed's. The singing, the shouts, the laughter, the play-acted rage was all intended for me. I, like all well-brought up new brides, allowed myself to be dragged around without uttering a word. I looked at the floor, a dumb, docile creature. The childish game held no amusement for me. I dreamed of disappearing, of being spirited away in the blink of an eye by some benign djinn, of rising up to the sky and landing in the place where Marvoud and Massouda were waiting. I saw myself as extinguished, annihilated, an object with no soul or volition. I was imprisoned, and the walls of my cell were impregnable. I cried with abandon. Everyone attributed it to my virgin modesty and praised my excellent upbringing.

When Memed and I were alone, I started to remove the gems encrusted in my hair that made my head so heavy. He came over to help me. I let him do it, but when he reached out a hand to caress me, I stopped him immediately, screaming, 'Don't touch me!' At first he thought I was still following tradition: the young wife was supposed to be resistant to the first act of love, even to refuse it. It was up to the husband to overcome the distance between them, to quell her fears, to oblige the ignorant young girl to receive him. It was a rape of sorts, but it was tradition. So Memed tried to kiss me, and was horrified when I drew out the dagger I'd hidden beneath my clothes. I said, 'You're not touching me. You'll never touch me. I'd rather kill myself!' He jumped up, and was about to cry out.

I forced myself to stay calm. 'Why call the others?' I asked him. 'They'll blame me, of course, but they'll also despise you, and it won't change a thing. You will not touch me, Memed. You'll never know how my body is made, you'll never invade my privacy, you'll never touch my breasts or my sex. I won't give myself to you. I refuse you.'

'You've gone crazy, Rayhana!'

'Yes, I have.'

His face was filled with defeat. He couldn't begin to understand what had happened to the Rayhana he thought he knew.

'You're my wife, before God and men,' he managed to say.

'Yes, but I'm a wife who rejects the husband who was chosen for her, who will not submit to him, or offer him her body.'

He said, 'You know full well that our religion and our laws

forbid that,' but his head was already bowed.

'Yes, I know that. You men love to evoke religion and law, especially when they suit your purposes. I accept the requirements of the law, and I will accept the fires of hell, but I won't give myself to you!'

'But you know I love you, you know I've always loved you!'

'Your emotional declarations mean nothing to me!'

'I'll try to make you happy, I'll obey you in everything, I'll give you the most beautiful things. We're rich.'

'Your riches mean nothing to me!'

'What will people say about me? What will they think of you?'

'What people think means nothing to me!'

We didn't sleep that night. Memed moved about ceaselessly, getting up, walking around the tent, swinging his arms, murmuring fragmented, incomprehensible words. I followed him with my eyes, ever-attentive, ready to pierce my own heart rather than be burned at the stake of ancient tradition. He waited, listened for my breathing, to assure himself I was sleeping, then cleared his throat and resumed his walking and his murmuring. I kept track of him: I was ready, dagger poised beneath my pillow. I knew many of our friends wouldn't be sleeping either. They'd be waiting for what tradition demanded: the cries of the violated virgin, the young girl fighting to protect her treasure, her purity. The display represented innocence battling against the invasion of adult life, against the virility that, despite the screams, must always triumph. It was an eternal combat that ended with the grand finale and sacred accomplishment of the act of love, leading to children, family, the respect of others, a life. I didn't want that life. I'd scrubbed my name from destiny's scriptures. I was dead to all but one thing.

At dawn, Memed timidly touched my arm. His voice was hoarse, his features distorted, his eyes filled with pain. My heart was heavy, but there was nothing I could do. I had nothing to offer him. I knew what his friends would whisper, 'A man who can't dominate his wife on the first night will be dominated by her all his life.' I knew Memed loved me, I knew I was breaking something inside him. But I too had been betrayed, shattered, torn... even if he had no idea about any of it.

We went to my mother's tent. She was already awake, waiting. She asked no questions and didn't speak to Memed. He went away again without a word. I slumped down on a mat and immediately fell asleep, the dagger still hidden beneath my veil. After a short time, I was woken by shouts. I watched, stunned, as my mother threw a pure white sheet spotted with fake blood out to my friends, who were gathered outside. They began to sing and dance around it. It was the blood of purity, the proof I was a virgin, that I'd been brought up well, that my honour had never been sullied.

It was another day of people parading into my mother's tent. I had to keep my face hidden. My friends cooed softly and asked me how it had gone. 'Paradise,' whispered one who had recently married, and the others guffawed; the matrons gave them hard stares. I said nothing. I was elsewhere, marvelling at how ready my mother had been to lie, to create a new reality, at her relentless determination to make me appear respectable. She knew full well I was scarred for life and had no pretensions to happiness. All I wanted was to one day embrace the child I'd been forced to abandon. My mother and I swam in two separate seas: I didn't think we'd ever meet again, ever tackle the same waves. Perhaps we would never even look each other in the eye again.

In the evening, Memed came back, surrounded by his friends. My mother had sacrificed a camel and laid on a great feast. Again the whole camp was invited. The griots intoned the most beautiful Saharan hymns. The girls abandoned modesty for an evening and let their hair down: they danced all night, making moves that at normal times would have been considered inappropriate. They winked cheekily at the young men, who, emboldened by the atmosphere, wheeled around doing *guéras*, fierce and virile dances, and threw their sweat-soaked turbans at the feet of their admirers. Memed was dragged into the middle of the crowd to join in the dance. I stole glances at him. He seemed distraught. His face was serene and smiling, his voice steady, but I knew it was an act: he was making a supreme effort to hide his pain.

My mother didn't mix with the crowd, but she showed every woman who approached her the blood-stained sheet, the proof of my innocence. I didn't dare look at her. Finally she called me to her, behind the tents.

'You're another woman, now,' she told me. 'You're married to Memed. He has to stay quiet and accept the farce I've orchestrated, or he'll lose face. The tribe will laugh at him, his honour will be stained. You can tell him you were born on a Friday evening and you never had a hymen, tell him whatever you like. If he wavers I'll speak to him again, but

I think he'll stay silent. Personally, I feel liberated now. You were the halter at my throat. Tomorrow I'll go and visit one of my cousins in town. She's ill and I haven't seen her for years. I'll be gone for a few weeks. Attend to your husband, make sure he forgets about all this. Help him get his smile back, and give him a child, a proper one!'

I asked my mother no questions. I didn't want to spend any more time than I had to in her presence.

When Memed and I were alone in our tent again, he did not hold back, 'What your mother did today was a slap in the face that I alone feel, an insult that I alone am aware of. You refuse me, and your mother judges me incapable. She didn't look at me once, she didn't give me her hand like you would to a son. That whole insulting show! The blood that wasn't yours! I might be weak, but I don't deserve such contempt. What have I done for you and your mother to scorn me so?'

He kept repeating, 'Why? Why?' Then he lowered his head and cried softly.

I didn't know how to respond. My heart was heavy and I felt at fault. Memed had done nothing wrong and he was suffering, he was the inadvertent victim of a storm my mother had raised. He wasn't a leading player, but he'd been dragged into her game. All he'd done was want to marry me. He thought he'd won me in love's contest, thought the doors of happiness would now open for him, thought he'd gained love and a union that would ennoble him in the eyes of the tribe. He'd ended up lost, betrayed, suffering, and unable to understand why. He kept on crying, quietly. I'd never seen a man cry, I'd thought only women did it; our men didn't express their feelings openly, didn't allow their tears to flow or their hearts' desires to show. They either kept it all inside, or they went faraway to swallow their pain. Memed didn't hide. The tears flooded his face, his new turban and his *boubou*. In spite of myself, I felt the urge to comfort him, to pull him to me and hold his head, as you would a child. But he wasn't a child. He calmed himself, tried to hold back his whimpers, to make his voice even.

I felt an enormous fatigue, the over-riding urge to vomit out my guts and my secret. I told Memed everything, 'I'm lost to you, Memed. I am dead flesh that can no longer know happiness. I'll never be able to give it either. I'm soiled for life. I crossed the *wadi* of suffering, the place from which you can never return. I'm lost, Memed, you must understand that, to you and to everyone else.' Memed listened in silence, without interrupting me once or asking a single question. Only when the flow of my words slowed and I paused for a second, feeling choked, did he touch my arm. I took a deep breath, then continued. I no longer saw Memed in front of me but a procession of all my torments, my many hours of distress and fear during the time I'd lived by the sea with my mother shut off inside her own pain and sick pride, and with Massouda trying to stoke the weak flame of survival in me, and with the baby, wriggling in my arms and reaching out his little hands to seize the days and nights. How had I endured it? Why was I not already dead?

When I'd finished my story, I felt as if an immense burden had been lifted from me. The words had relieved some of my pain. I wasn't free, but I'd been able to lick my wounds.

Memed was no longer crying, just trembling a little. He got up and went outside. I watched him through the gaps in the tent, pacing around, turning his head to the east, absorbed, asking counsel of the stars perhaps, or the light wind that caressed the tents, or the sleeping compound. Perhaps he was praying to God to show him the path. I knew he would speak to no one about it, that he would keep my secret, but now he was obliged to act. I awaited his verdict, which seemed a foregone conclusion to me. I'd been so clear, I'd said, 'I don't belong to you, I can't belong to you, though I know you have good qualities. I won't belong to you, because I don't belong to myself and I don't want to belong to anyone else.' He would announce our divorce tomorrow, and I would have to return to my mother's tent, to suffer her silence and her scorn. It wouldn't kill me, I'd get through the long nights one by one, then one day the sun might shine again, I might see my lost flesh and blood again, I might learn to smile again... I was almost happy with the turn of events: it meant I could reclaim my solitude. Having already been married, no one could impose anything more on me. It's all written, I thought, everything that has happened and everything still to come. I had always been at the mercy of fate, just a small atom, spinning inside the immense whirlwind of the Sahara.

Finally Memed returned. By the light of the moon that filtered into the tent, I saw a new resolution in his eyes. He said, 'You've suffered greatly. You bled and you stayed silent, and none of us saw your hidden wounds. I understand everything now, and I want to heal your pain. I'll go and find your child. I'll bring him to the town first, then I'll bring him here. I'll say I found him abandoned and have decided to adopt him. That way he can live with us. I'll love him as if he were my own son.' I was stupefied. Memed came over and embraced me. I didn't push him away. My heart beat hard, as if it was trying to escape. I felt the dampness of his tears, heard his breathing. My body was silent, but my heart spoke. My arms slowly opened to him. I let Memed take what he thought was his right.

I was filled with anxiety at first. How could I find my son in this muddle of streets that lead nowhere, people roaming blindly towards destinations I couldn't guess at, women standing with bags on their shoulders waiting for I don't know who, bedraggled children who reached their hands out towards me, old people begging for a coin, adolescents grinning foolishly, veils in every colour of the rainbow, *boubous* blowing in the wind, tailored suits, drivers with vacant eyes, gripping their steering wheels and looking straight ahead, empty faces, bashed up old cars and shining new ones, faded houses and colours? What if I too lost myself completely? I felt, dizzy, nauseous, my heart was in my mouth, and everywhere I smelled decay. There was something rotting in the stinking, polluted air, and something dead in people's faces. Despite all the lights, I felt an absence of light. The night was as dark as the ghosts that strolled aimlessly along the avenues.

Hama had explained it to me: this was not my native '*badiya*', my desert, nor was it Atar, but a whole other world, another life with everything right up against everything else. It had to be viewed differently; you had to speak and act differently. Most importantly of all, you had to always be on guard: never show what you were carrying, never trust strangers... He told me that people here didn't know each other, not even their neighbours, that the city was a melting pot of individuals from all sorts of different places, who sometimes even forgot wherever it was they'd come from, and just created new relationships, new camps. Sometimes there was no place for emotions. Hama warned me of thousands of dangers and sought to inoculate me against all of them. His advice made Mbarka's endless instructions seem tame.

Hama's sister lived in Ksar. 'It's a good area,' Hama said, 'not one of the over-crowded parts crammed with poor people and cockroaches, and not one of the fancy areas with rich people and mosquitoes, but somewhere between the two. It has the right balance: small business owners, middle-ranking public officials, Moroccan restaurants, Senegalese garages...' The house seemed very grand to me. It had a large courtyard, a never-ending hall, many rooms and staircases. There were objects everywhere.

Hama's sister, Hawa, met us with sweet words and gracious gestures. She was around forty, with a high forehead and smiling, slightly slanted eyes. She was quite plump, but her long veil hung elegantly over her curves. Her skin looked white, but I could discern a darker shade blooming beneath. I was swiftly drowned in a stream of welcomes. I hadn't anticipated any kind of welcome at all, but I saw that Hawa idolised her brother and had thought for a moment that he might have changed his persuasion and be bringing a girlfriend or a fiancé to meet her. He quickly disabused her of this, explaining, 'She's a little sister, the sister of a very dear friend of mine. She lost a fortune and hopes to find it again here. I've just come to get her settled, help her to acclimatise, then I'll entrust her to you and get back to my Atar. I can't bear

138

this fake city.'

I didn't sleep that night. I worried about what the next day might have in store, in this city I'd been told was merciless, where life could slap you down and no one would even bother to look. I was afraid of what might befall me in such an enormous camp of stone and cement, where nothing was quiet yet nothing ever spoke to me. I trembled to think that my lost love could be hidden somewhere in this chaos of soulless dwellings and lives, that the sneers of heartless city people might have wiped away his smile.

My eyes refused to close. I ached from the long journey and the jolting of the minibus we'd taken, much more violent than the movements of the most disobedient camel. I'd been given a narrow room with a large bed. I didn't know how to sleep in such a big bed, and I wasn't sure where to put the drum. I finally wrapped it in an old blanket I found and hid it under the bed. I looked around the room and felt my solitude keenly. I was even more isolated than I'd been with my mother and Massouda. The things around me seemed lifeless, as if I was lost in a silent jungle. There were sounds everywhere – lorries, cars backfiring, horns, distant music, shouting – but they didn't stir anything in me. Nothing was talking to me, not like in our desert, or even in Atar, where you would pay attention if something spoke during the night, because that sound was going somewhere.

My last night at the camp appeared to me as if in a dream: my farewell to my childhood and the prisons that had held me; my dissent and revolt; my insult to my tribe. I had no regrets; in fact I breathed fully as if to inhale more deeply the memory of how I'd affronted them just when they thought they'd subdued me, conquered me through the weight of their numbers and the hearth they'd tied me to.

Memed had returned from the city alone. He bowed his head and couldn't meet my eye. He went to his mother's tent, talked with his friends, about nothing, I knew, for it was just to delay coming to me. Then finally he entered the tent, complained of being very tired and lay down to sleep. He was obviously distraught. 'I'll tell you tomorrow,' he mumbled, 'tomorrow.' But burning lava flowed through me. It devoured my heart, twisted around my guts. My throat choked with pride and fire, my eyes were blind to everything but the little being he'd promised he'd bring back to me. I couldn't bear Memed's silence. I shook him violently and shouted, 'Where's my child?'

He lifted his head and sat up. He hadn't been asleep, and as always when he felt he'd failed, he was on the brink of tears. He looked at me as if he was seeing me for the first time and thought I might fly away and leave him at any moment. He was visibly afraid, of me and of the rest of the world.

'Where's my child?' I repeated.

'I went there, my life,' he replied, tentatively. 'I went to town and hired the sturdiest car I could find, with the most experienced driver, and we went to look for the child. We drove around the desert until we found the Imraguen camp, but Massouda wasn't there. We went to all the neighbouring camps – I never knew there were so many – and finally we found her. I took her to one side and spoke to her. She was frightened and trembling. She refused to say anything at first. I had to swear over and over that I was your husband and was there on your behalf. She told me your mother had come by, in a car with another woman and someone else from your family, driven by a black driver who didn't speak our language, and she'd taken the child. She said he was going somewhere cleaner and safer. She gave Massouda a lot of money, the price of her silence. Massouda said she would be silent but she couldn't take the money; she loved the boy too much to be paid for him.'

I was no longer listening; my ears were closed to Memed's excuses and laments. I was beyond all that, had moved to a place of suffering and hate. I was the lioness whose cub had been taken. I was ready to confront my mother, but she still hadn't returned. That was when I made the decision to escape them all, to leave and look for Marvoud myself, to search for a thousand years if that was what it took. I left the tent, unveiled, my head and body aflame. Memed begged me not to go. I did not turn back. He didn't have the strength to follow me. He cried, but I didn't care about his tears, he was finished for me. I walked, delirious, to the centre of the camp, tears in my eyes, flames in my belly, murmuring curses. I went straight to the chief's tent. Everything was calm, as if the earth had not just trembled under my feet. The drum sat on its spears; their voice, their story, their idol. The *rezzam* that housed their pride would never sound for me, the *Reytamas*[23] would not come and make it rumble to find my son. Lost animals, perhaps, but not the little soul they'd stolen from me. I decided then and there to snatch their sacred fetish from them, to emasculate them. That would be my final message to their idiotic pride. I would take their name and lose myself in the black night, confront the hydras of the city, search until I found my own flesh and blood, and never return.

---

23 Author's note: Tribe traditionally charged with maintaining the drum.

Morning found me still dazed, tangled in my dreams. My eyes and body were heavy from lack of sleep, and I was filled with anxiety about what was to come. Hawa's morning calls to awaken the household rang in my ears like a gong, but the light streaming through the windows began to revive me. I went downstairs to find Hama and his sister in a comfortable living room furnished with armchairs, sofas, divans and rugs. I'd never seen such luxurious furniture. A young girl came in. She acknowledged me without looking at me, flopped down on a divan and demanded coffee. A servant brought in a sumptuous breakfast: croissants, rolls, eggs, oranges, other things I didn't even know the names of. The girl held a mobile phone to her ear and talked to herself as if she were possessed. Sometimes she smiled, or burst out laughing. When she finally put the phone down to eat, she still kept her eye on its screen.

'Those things are an illness,' Hama said. 'Coumba,' he scolded, 'aren't you going to greet our guest?' The girl got up and came over lazily. She held out a soft hand, mumbled a barely-perceptible, 'Hello.'

Hama and I had only tea and bread. I noticed Hama's body language had become more decisive, his voice more grounded. He was clearly playing a different character, someone more like an uncle and a brother: his sister's house was not the place to flout convention. I wanted to tell him I liked the other Hama better, Mbarka's friend, but I didn't dare.

Hama's sister left the room and came back with her arms full of clothes: two colourful veils, two long, silky dresses, high-heeled shoes. I didn't want to accept them. She said, 'But look how you're dressed, child, you'll bring shame on us!

I can't let you stay in my house dressed like that. You have to wear these clothes, you have no choice.' Hama gave me a wink. I understood that Hawa's instructions were not up for discussion.

Hama opened his bag and brought out my jewellery. 'These are to pay her way,' he told his sister.

'Why's she getting rid of her jewellery? She doesn't need money here. As long as she stays in my house, she'll want for nothing.'

Her look was severe, her tone brusque, as if we'd offended her. I made myself as small as I could.

'It's her sister who asked me to do it,' said Hama. 'To sell them and give Rayhana the money, so she can buy herself things.'

Hawa seized the jewellery from him. She looked at it, weighed it in her hands and announced a sum.

'That's very fair,' said Hama. He turned and gave me another wink.

A few minutes later a young man of around twenty came in. His tight trousers and loose shirt revealed a lean, hair-covered body. He had black glasses and a well-groomed moustache, coarse, springy hair and mischievous eyes. His polite smile grew brighter the moment he saw Hama. He cried, 'Uncle!' They embraced warmly. Hama's sister watched her son with a disapproving air. When the outpourings of affection were over, she addressed him sternly, 'Nice to finally see you. You were out all night again, weren't you? You forget your studies, and me, and your sister. And you run around all day, who knows where!'

'I'm with friends, Mum. I go to the university every day,

and I work a bit too.'

'You, work? You've never got one *ouguiya* on you.'

'I'm doing a traineeship, actually.'

'In what?'

'Journalism. I want to be a journalist.'

'But you're studying law!'

'Law can lead to anything. I want to be a journalist and a lawyer. I'm going to know the law and explain it through journalism.'

'All these big words and never anything concrete! What about your exams? They're coming up soon, aren't they?'

'I'm preparing for them, Mother.'

'So you should be! What if you fail them again?'

The young man muttered something indecipherable and made a dismissive gesture with his hand, but his mother was already on her way out. 'I'm going to the market. Look after our guest!'

Hama took his nephew aside and spoke to him. I tried to catch snippets of the conversation. The young man nodded his head and repeated, 'OK, OK.' He turned to look at me. I crossed my arms over my chest, feeling scrutinised. Hama called me over. I went to them. I felt nervous and small, as if they were about to decide my fate.

'I'll be leaving soon,' said Hama, 'this town makes me dizzy. I'll go crazy if I stay any longer. I don't know anyone here any more, and my business is calling me back to Atar.'

I didn't ask what business that was. A shiver travelled down my back and into my limbs.

'I'm not abandoning you,' Hama went on, as if to address my unspoken fear. Abdou here is my nephew. I love him very much, he knows the city and its people well, he's intelligent and streetwise. He'll be able to help you. I'd only be a burden. I'm not used to this place any more. Besides,' he added, laughing, 'I'm too visible.'

'You're in good hands,' said Abdou. His eyes caressed me. 'You'll want for nothing. You'll feel at home here in no time.'

I didn't like his playful tone, or his insistent look, or his false smile.

'I want to find my son,' I said.

'We'll find him,' Abdou replied. His firmness reassured me a little.

'I'll check in with you every day,' said Hama. 'And Mbarka will come and join you if that turns out to be necessary. Don't be frightened. You have friends who love you and will always be there for you.'

The next day, Hama took me to the market. I bought myself new veils, dresses, shoes, and also one of the latest mobile phones. It was exciting, but I vowed never to become a prisoner to the thing like Hama's niece was, always talking even though she was alone, and forgetting to be polite. The electronics market was a crazy place, piled with telephones, computers, so many modern gadgets, both new and used. Hama told me it was known as *Noghta Sakhina,* Hot Point, the same name as an Al Jazeera programme on TV that covered deaths all over the world. There were stalls made of planks of wood, faces staring out from them, arms reaching out forcefully to offer you improbable objects, voices hailing you in the narrow alleyways where everyone was pressed together: sellers, shoppers, passers-by, but also, Hama warned me, pickpockets, thieves and people who were selling nothing but tall tales. How did people manage to live in the midst of such a crush? How could you be yourself amongst so many other people? I began to understand why they used to say at the camp that city people had no spirit: no malice, but also no heart. It was because they never had any time alone with themselves. The crowd penetrated right inside them. It stole their spirit and tainted their thoughts. This mass of humanity, the faces and the shouting, stayed with you even after you'd been away from them for a few hours, eaten a meal, met friends. You still heard the murmur of the crowd in your ears, and without even realising it, you began to behave as the crowd did.

Hama said that to blend in as a city girl I had to look clean, pretty and modern. He took me to see a friend of his called Halima. She was a large, busty woman with very black skin. Her face was ravaged by what must have been smallpox and she wore a plain, loose dress, but she had a ravishing smile. She took me to a hammam. I watched as the top layer of my skin disappeared, taking with it black streaks of grime I'd never noticed was there. Another large woman, with a foreign accent, fumed at the mess that was my hair, roundly insulted my previous hairdressers and, declaring half of my strands to be dead, chopped them clean off. I was afraid to protest in case she slapped me. My nails were also examined and sacrificed, my eyebrows re-designed, my face painted. I looked in a mirror and didn't like what I saw. 'There,' said the woman, 'her beauty's starting to show itself!' She embraced me warmly and I had to promise to come back again soon.

Before Hama left town he gave me a lot of money. 'Spend it carefully,' he said, 'and don't forget to always be on your guard – they're monsters, the people of your tribe.' My heart came to my mouth when, as a farewell, he took my chin and shook it, as if I were a little girl. I grabbed the fold of his *boubou* and failed to hold back my tears of love for him, for Mbarka, even for old Fatmouha. He forced himself to be cheerful, saying, 'You'll find your child, and you'll be back with us again before you know it.'

Abdou explained what he called his strategy, 'I'll pretend to be a journalist. I sort of am one anyway, because they've promised me a traineeship at a private radio station very soon. I've got a card a friend gave me, look. It says, 'Journalist'. OK, it's not a real one, but no one knows the difference. You'll be my assistant, a trainee. I'll get a microphone you can hold. Do you know how to do that?'

'I don't even know what one is.'

'I'll teach you. You'll follow me everywhere. I'll do the talking, you just stay quiet. OK?'

We began with the orphanages. We went to the edges of the city, to places where the ground was cracking under the weight of people and mountains of waste. The paving on the roads was disappearing and the dunes could be seen underneath. The houses bowed their heads, unable to hide behind showy city disguises. Cement replaced planks, splendour had long since past, and the look in people's eyes betrayed the slow death of their ambitions.

I trembled on the threshold of a large house from which the shouts of children could be heard. A man with a wild beard blocked our path. Behind him I could see children playing in a large courtyard, all of them older than my son would be. Their clothes were faded but clean. Sometimes they glanced towards us. I thought I could read appeal in their eyes. I reached out my hand instinctively. The bearded man wouldn't let us pass.

'Who are you? What have you come for?'

Abdou lifted his chin. He said, 'We're journalists.'

The man's voice softened. 'Wait a minute,' he said. He closed the door and left us in the street.

'Did you see the children?' I cried. 'They're lovely! How could anyone abandon those little things? And why's the man sending us away?'

'He'll come back. But don't forget: I'm the one asking the questions. You take the opportunity to have a good look around in case you see your son.'

I closed my eyes and prayed quietly that God would help me rediscover my little lost love, and that these children would find the love they must be missing so much. 'That rough man knows nothing of tenderness,' I told Abdou. He placed a finger to his lips, commanding me to be silent.

The door opened again, to a young man with a tranquil bearing. He welcomed us in. We passed through the courtyard, now empty of children, and were swallowed by a dark corridor that led to a door decorated with holy verses. The room within held a desk, two armchairs and a divan. There was calligraphy I couldn't decipher on the walls. Abdou sat down opposite the man. At a sign from him, I held out the microphone. I paid no attention to Abdou's questions or the man's answers. My heart was beating hard. Would we see any more children? I understood now that this was a charitable organisation that picked up abandoned children and gave them food

148

and education. It survived on donations which it had to use carefully. 'What about smiles?' I wanted to ask, 'and kisses on cheeks and the tops of heads, and hugs?' I remembered what Abdou had told me and held my tongue.

The director showed us round the orphanage. There were three rooms and eighteen children in total. Toddlers gazed at us, clung to us with their looks, implored us to give them even a scrap of love. I wanted to cry. I had no happiness to offer them. We saw mattresses squeezed together on the floor, limp cushions and piles of rags. Wooden tablets with the letters of the alphabet drawn on them leaned against the bare walls. There was a bucket of water, a plate containing the remains of a meal. Nothing was clean, everything smelled stale and sad. The children were aged between three and six. They intoned verses from the Quran. The smallest ones played quietly with new toys and stuck close to their carers, young veiled women who didn't lift their heads when Abdou addressed them. They answered his questions in a monotone, as briefly as they could, 'The children are well behaved, thanks be to God, yes, a paediatrician comes to see them, yes they study the alphabet and the Quran, no cases of serious illness.' The director intervened, 'When it comes to adoption, we make sure first of all that the family is morally respectable, has a solid reputation, is Muslim and has the means to provide for the child's needs...'

We went to other orphanages too. They were all very similar. The orphans had the same fearful eyes, their expressions lost in looks that slid away. There was the same stench of abandonment, the same sound of children reciting words from sacred texts, or crying for long-lost loved-ones. There were the same directors with long beards and tired phrases, the same carers who didn't offer hugs.

I grew full of rage at the world and its false gods. 'People talk about goodness, they pray and bow down before the Good Lord, they debate holy truths, and all the time these innocent little souls are forgotten!'

Abdou didn't understand. 'But there are orphanages everywhere!' he replied.

'Not where I'm from, it would be impossible,' I replied. 'It would be unimaginable: every soul belongs to a tribe, and there are always neighbours, friends, relatives, travellers. A child would never be left alone, without a tent to shelter it, without a family!' Abdou shrugged his shoulders, as if to say, 'Where you come from, they stole your child.' He was right. I no longer knew where my hate was directed. I nodded and said, 'Yes, it's true, they hollowed me out, they stole a precious treasure from me, but children aren't abandoned there. They're not left in the hands of faceless organisations, there's always a tribe, even if it's a wandering one, a family, even if it's a starving one, a Massouda, even if she gets over-ruled. There's always someone. The first person who passes, the first to hear the tears, the first camp.'

When we'd visited all the orphanages, we weren't sure what to do next. We tried social services, then the hospitals. Abdou sent out enquiries through his friends in the press. There was nothing, not even the slightest sign.

It was decided that I should stay at home while Abdou continued the search. 'You get in my way,' he said simply. So I was left to pace around the house, waiting for the phone to ring and announce my deliverance. I helped with the housework, watched endless soap operas, listened to the chattering of the maid, of which I understood nothing, and pored over the story of my own life. I dwelled especially on the hours I'd spent with Marvoud, the time when his tiny fists had kneaded my face and my breasts, when he'd sucked, unaware of any ugliness in the world, when he'd stared wide-eyed, as if marvelling at it all. Would he recognise me today? I was crazy to think he would.

Abdou asked me for money every day, for his shopping, his research. I thought I should put aside a small amount for myself, to help me escape if I found my son. But I didn't understand money, and Abdou seemed insatiable. In the end, I gave everything I had to Hawa. She was happy with the arrangement, saying, 'Don't worry, I'll make sure you're sensible.'

'Give Abdou whatever he needs when he asks for it,' I told her. Abdou grumbled, but he was too afraid of his mother to protest too much.

Coumba suddenly found her tongue and began to speak to me. All she ever talked about was her love life, the boys she liked, the relationships she was having via her computer. I tried to argue that to know someone was to feel, see and hear them, that it was the internal murmuring of something, that it was... I didn't know myself how to find the words I needed, but I knew friendship and love weren't pictures inside a machine. Coumba laughed at me. I often envied her the simple joy that could light up her face, the happiness she was able to access, her carefreeness, even her naivety. She had everything: a roof, a family, smiles around her, a mother... I had a mother too, of course, but... I didn't allow myself to give any further thought to what my life might have been, here or elsewhere, if I'd had a different mother.

Mbarka and Hama called often. I grabbed for the phone as if it were a life belt, grasped it tightly and pressed it hard to my ear. Mbarka bombarded me with advice. I only really heard the music of her voice, drawing warmth and comfort from it. It was as if she reached inside me and took away some of my distress. 'No, my sister,' I told her, 'tribes are not in charge here. No one's in charge. These people have no brands for their beasts, no names in their heads, no past in their veins. No, there are so many different people, from all the regions of the country, and none of them know the language of the heart. There are so many houses, so many tall buildings, but no real roofs, no tents that provide support and shelter. There are crowds in every street, but never anyone around you, people don't see you. I can't wait to find my child and get out of here… no, don't be afraid, my tribe doesn't exist here.'

But I was wrong: my tribe did exist. The innumerable noises of the city drowned out its voice, the dense mists masked its features, but it appeared one day when Abdou made an unexpected move. His research having come to a dead end, he'd decided to explore new avenues. He went to see Mahjoub, Memed's uncle, the rich man of our tribe. He introduced himself as a student hoping to write a memoir of the history and customs of the Oulad Mahmoud. He was undercover, with a new identity, new name, even a new face, because he'd let his beard grow.

'You're crazy,' I told him, 'you don't know them! When they find out, they'll kill you!'

'They can't do anything to me,' he said. 'This isn't their desert. Thanks to you, I'm exploring a form of journalism that's

not very widespread here. It's called investigative journalism.
I will not only uncover the secrets of your people, and find
out where they're hiding your baby, I'll also write an article, a
series of articles perhaps, that have wider significance. Then,
finally, I'll be a real journalist. The editors will open their
doors to me then.'

Abdou sometimes looked at me a bit too intently. He liked
to tell stories in which the beautiful heroine had my name
and the amorous suitor bore an uncanny resemblance to him.
He talked about an impenetrable world that he could show
me, full of grand and powerful people, also of unimagined
distant countries. It reminded me of Yahya's bragging. Why
did they all try to dazzle me with smoke and mirrors? Abdou
should have known that I'd left the land of illusions, that I'd
already spent a long time wandering in places of real pain,
that my eyes had been opened and that all I now saw when
people described wonders to me were painful shadows. He did
remain discreet in his approaches, even when he made himself
obvious. Sometimes he would brush my hand in passing, very
lightly, as if testing the waters, sometimes he would throw a
tender word into the middle of a sentence, sometimes I felt he
was kissing me with a look. I always behaved as if I hadn't
noticed. There was no malice in his advances, and there was
probably sincerity behind his boasts. I knew I could put a stop
to it if it went too far. I tried not to give him any cause for
confusion. From the beginning I referred to him as my brother.
I spoke about the death of my dreams and repeated often that
there could be no love in me other than that for my little lost
soul.

Abdou also spoke about his studies. Law, he told me, could unlock happiness for people. Modern law, he explained, was quite simply justice. Each person was entitled to their own truth, their own belongings. Each person contributed what they could, and everyone could live beneath the same tent, but without anyone intruding on anyone else's space. 'Each person,' he said, excluded no one. His ideas seemed strange to me. At the camp, we didn't want to be 'each person', we wanted to be 'all', even if the chief was a little more 'all' than the rest of us. We were one because the tribe was one body. Abdou hated tribes and tribalism. He called it one of the worst ills of the country. I listened and silently disagreed. Despite what they'd put me through, my people remained, in my heart, my people. I hated them, but I still felt the invisible chord that could stretch and stretch until it surrounded us all. I'd stolen their drum, but I belonged to them a bit all the same. As soon as I had that thought, I was appalled: I belonged to them. Why didn't I belong to myself? What race does a person belong to if they reject their camp and their relatives and leave?

Abdou seemed stunned by my 'idiocies', laughed at my contradictions. It was true, I had no idea where the path to certainty was, but the complicated language Abdou used condemned me to always get it wrong. I was reminded of the teacher. What had he ever gained by isolating himself? I was even more alone now, though, than he had been. I didn't know what to think. As always when I found it hard to reflect on something, I left the questions hanging.

Above all, Abdou wanted to be a journalist. He wanted to sweep away the old certainties that hid the old secrets, and denounce injustice using the law. That was what he told me anyway. His sister sometimes scoffed that he was full of empty words, that she'd never seen any articles by him. He said she didn't know anything, sometimes he wrote things under a different name, or the editors wouldn't publish what he wrote because they were corrupt, controlled by the people in power. All that would change one day, he said, thanks partly to him.

When I felt anxious, I took the *rezzam* out of the suitcase where I'd stashed it alongside Abdou's books, and questioned it, 'How many people have lost their lives because of you? How many souls departed to protect you? In all our battles men died clustered around you. You were their beating heart, their sacred pennant, the sound of their courage, the blood in their veins. To lose you is to taste the bitter fruit of defeat. Without you, the battle must end because it no longer has any meaning. You were the totem, the one our girls sang to:

> *Speak, rezzam*
> *You have no cares*
> *Nothing can touch you*
> *Except our own hands*

The ungraspable *rezzam*, the untouchable *rezzam*, the *rezzam* sitting proud on the strong spears outside the chief's house, maintained by the *Reytamas*, proud servants to the idol-drum. There you are, *rezzam*, in my small hands, wrapped in a dirty sheet, buried in a battered old suitcase, alongside some foolish books. You're mute, your magnificence is silenced, all because your people, those who are ready to die for you, to protect you from ferocious attacks, the fury of other tribes, every possible evil, never expected a young girl, her heart enflamed by pain and harbouring all the love in the world, to disappear into the black night carrying in her feeble arms the weight of the legends that had flayed her.'

One night, I saw Yahya on the television. It felt as if he'd stepped out of the box and was looking at me. He was just the same: his smile, the way he nodded his head, his calculating silence and those round eyes that fixed you straight on, without shame. He was challenging me, laughing at my failure. I couldn't contain myself; I let out a curse that made Abdou turn.

'What?'

'No, nothing, it's just… that man…'

'He's an important engineer,' Abdou explained. 'He was working for a foreign organisation, and he helped to discover a major deposit of gold. Now he's been offered a senior position at the Ministry of Mining. Very intelligent! What a future he's got ahead of him!'

I listened, stunned, as Yahya spoke. I understood nothing of what he said, but he was full of confidence, and the journalist interviewing him clearly respected him. He wore a European suit, glasses and that false smile I knew so well. Something bitter rose up in my throat. I rushed to the toilet, to vomit and cry.

I marvelled at how such hyenas could be praised to the skies. Yahya was admired by everyone. What could I ever expect from a world that lauded those who violated people's trust and their dreams? 'A great man, a senior official, he has a future.' I wanted to run into the street and shout that he was an ogre, that he'd deceived me and was about to deceive the whole world. They'd think I was crazy, my tribe would find me, and that would be the end for my little lost soul, I'd never see him again. And had I not sworn to erase Yahya from my mind, had I not torn him out from inside me?

He's not the father of my son, I repeated to myself, Marvoud was born of my own naivety and my greedy senses. I repeated to myself, 'Yahya does not exist, Yahya is dead,' to try to exorcise the demons.

Abdou climbed straight into the jaws of the beast. When he came back, he was laughing. 'I spied on them for you and they paid me for it. They kept slipping crumpled notes into my pocket, "For your studies". They're hoping to see their tribe and its myths glorified, they want to be able to read all about their absurd pride in a book. That would be real posterity, a book. They cajoled me, pampered me, bribed me. But I'm never going to write that book. For me it is only the law, the law and journalism. And Rayhana too,' he added softly, letting his hand float towards my breast. I dodged his caress and encouraged him with a smile to carry on with his research. 'It's extraordinary,' he told me, 'that these Bedouins can remain what they are while at the same time playing the game of being modern. They travel. They go all the way to China to bring back products. They use the internet, they work with the state, the tax system, they cultivate political relationships, they pay journalists and administrators. Sometimes they even live in grand villas. Then, in the blink of an eye, when they're resting or when they leave the city – and they leave whenever they can – they become what they were again, what they want to be,

Bedouins, people of the desert.'

Every evening I waited for news of the camp, clues that would help me recover my heart. I began to dare to hope that I'd finally found the path that would set me free, end my wandering, secure my victory against the forces of evil. But these moments of elation were often followed by discouragement. Abdou was at the heart of things, he said. But which things? It was the story of the tribe he was being given, the story of our eponymous ancestor who was abandoned in the middle of the desert by people who wanted to exterminate his family, who survived because a camel came out of the shadows and allowed him to drink its milk, because a pure spring sprang up beneath his feet, because a marabout with a white beard appeared before him every morning to show him the way. Our ancestor naturally grew good and strong, eliminated his tribal enemies and founded our lineage. 'That's all it is,' I insisted to Abdou. 'I can tell you hundreds of our legends. We learn them when we're born, we drink them at our mothers' breasts, they surround us, our stories, we make poems out of them and we all recite them. Legend, that's all it is!'

'No, wait,' he told me, 'I'm not clear about everything yet. Wait a little. Soon they'll let me inside their houses. Your son must be there. They'll have given him a new name, a new lineage, but I'll recognise him. I'll know him when I see him, I promise.'

Impatience began to burrow away at me. Doubts assailed my spirit. Was Abdou really on my side? I learned that Bedouins were like birds of prey, that they dressed in city garbs but deep down remained what they were, but how did that advance my cause, how did it help me recover what they'd stolen from me? I could see that Abdou's sense of purpose was becoming blunted, the threads of his craft, as he put it, had got tangled up in his mind. He no longer spoke about law and journalism, but came home with pieces of paper on which he'd written little poems dictated by someone from the tribe, which he recited loudly. He was delighted by the culture of poetry, so common in the camps, so new to him.

Had he forgotten me? I wondered whether his encounters with this offshoot of my tribe were starting to excite him, he who was so stubbornly 'anti-tribalist'. But he also brought me news from the camp, things he'd heard whispered when people forgot he was there or thought he wasn't listening. I heard that Memed had left the camp, deserted our tents not long after me, gone, it seemed, to lick his wounds in some foreign country. I learned that my mother no longer spoke to anyone and never left her tent. They said she'd been driven crazy by the loss of her husband, her daughter and her honour. My uncle had publicly declared my blood to be traitor's blood, which meant that with no fear of vengeance from my tribe, with its blessing in fact, I could now be murdered by anyone in broad daylight. The young people of the camp had slashed their arms on the spears that had held the drum and sworn to bring it back one day. The girls, my friends, had refused to marry until the drum was recovered.

I had a good laugh at all of it. Their pain was nothing to mine. They'd lost a drum; an object was no longer in its proper place. I had a crater in my soul. Only reunion with my child would fill the void.

'When they return Marvoud to me, I'll return their drum,' I said to Abdou one day.

'Do they even know Marvoud exists?' he replied. 'It was your mother…'

'It was all of them,' I retorted. 'The whole tribe stole my son. It was their vanity, their arrogance, their false truths. They all need to face up to it.'

They rang the bell politely, but behind the ringing I sensed a kind of dissonance, a mute, smothered rage, a rupture in the order of things. I wanted to warn Abdou, but he'd already opened the door to them. They sprung on him immediately and started to beat him. 'Where is the bitch?' they shouted. Hawa and Coumba woke, terrified, and began to scream. I hid myself in a tiny space, hardly visible, beneath the stairs, tense with fear. I heard Abdou shouting, 'You won't find her here, she's left!' They didn't stay for long. They took a quick look into the bedrooms, then pushed Abdou out in front of them, ignoring his mother's and his sister's protests. 'He's a thief and a terrorist,' they yelled. 'We'll take him to the police, he'll tell us where she's hiding and we'll find her. She stole our tribal drum and our women's jewellery. We'll find her, wherever she is!' When they'd gone, I came out of my hiding place, dishevelled and trembling. Coumba and her mother were crying and pulling at their hair. I said nothing to them, just grabbed the suitcase that contained my trophy and Abdou's books, and disappeared into the night. I dragged my defeated, bleeding soul out into the city of ghosts. How had Abdou managed to fall into their trap? Why had he revealed himself? Or had he simply done a deal with them? I was helpless, shattered. I had nowhere to go.

The dust of the day, the fragrances of the night, the weak light coming from the tired street lights, the fluorescent glow of the kiosks that remained open, all muddled together that evening to give the impression of a vague mist. I walked through it without registering anything, like a machine propelled by an external force. I knew I was beaten: the doors to hope had slammed shut. All I had left was one burden, the huge suitcase, which I could no longer carry: I tried it on one shoulder, on the other shoulder, on my head. Sometimes, moaning, I even left it on the road. It was no longer the cursed drum, it was no longer Abdou's books, it was the coffin for my strangled hope that I was dragging behind me. I didn't shed a tear. Images paraded past me, wavering in my mind's eye: Messouda, Mbarka, Hama, Marvoud, whose smile I could no longer conjure up. A vanished world. The faces evaporated, forever perhaps. I'd been defeated. I railed out loud against fate, my mother, my uncle, the tribe, the entire country, myself. The rare passers-by turned to look, then walked quickly away from me, thinking me possessed. No road suggested itself to me and I took no decisions. I wandered aimlessly through the silent night-time city.

A man came near me, slowed, matched my erratic steps for a while, then continued on his way. A group of young men called out to me, then disappeared. I was nothing, not really visible. With every step, my arms threatened to drop my useless burden. They'd carried the drum so bravely, back when I'd seen signs, however small, of a presence, a promise, back when I could still recall the features of Marvoud. They'd taken the weight of the damned totem then! Now everything had been erased. My body would no longer co-operate. My path, already rocky, had become unusable, obstructed by the gaping jaws of great predators: my mother, my uncle, my tribe, Yahya, the world.

I didn't know the alleyways I was taking, knew only that I had to stay away from the big avenues. I edged along grimy, crumbling passageways. Suddenly I thought I was somewhere I knew. I looked around and recognised Halima's hammam. I stopped walking. I don't know why. Perhaps because I'd wandered for long enough, perhaps because I was sick of always running, perhaps because nothing mattered any more.

The hammam and the shops around it were closed, the road deserted. A weak street light attempted to give life to a drab, depressing scene. Colourless shadows danced on the surface of stagnant waters. I wasn't afraid because I had no future left and was stripped bare. My back was aching too much to ignore. I placed the suitcase on the ground and sat on it. I would wait for dawn. Perhaps tomorrow… I no longer knew what I wanted from tomorrow.

A shadow approached me. An old man with a straggly white beard. He wore a dirty jacket and carried a club in his hand.

'What are you doing here?'

I had no answer. I managed to make a sound – a sob. He immediately hid the club behind his back and addressed me in a gentler tone, 'What are you doing here, child?

'I'm waiting for morning,' I said.

'It will come. Without fail. And then?'

'I'll see Halima.'

'Ah, Halima! She always comes early; she lights the fire for the hammam. But why don't you go to her house?'

'I don't know where she lives. That's why I'm waiting here.'

'I see, my child, you've come from a long way away. From Charg, I'm sure of it.'

I nodded my head to avoid having to respond.

'I knew it. We people from Charg always arrive very late, then we wait for the morning. That's how it is, we wait for the morning. Ah yes, we're always waiting. The rain, the grass, the soft wind, we wait. We respect things and we know how to wait for time to pass. People from Charg are not like other people, so quick to seize the rainy season before it's arrived, so greedy to taste the udder of the ewe before she's even given birth. Yes, the people of Charg take time as it comes. I had camels, cows and sheep once, you know. They're all gone. Pfft! Two years without rain and everything was gone. So I came to the town, very late at night, and I waited for morning, just like you, sitting on my suitcase, just like you. And now I've been the night watchman here for twenty years and I'm still waiting. I don't complain, that's just the way it is. You can't complain about the will of God, can you?'

I nodded again. I didn't have the energy to listen to him properly. Anger and remorse had stolen my hearing. I'd abandoned Abdou. What had happened to him? Where had my people taken him? To one of their houses? To a police station?

Would they torture him until he confessed? What did he have to tell them? Nothing they didn't already know. They'd want to know where I was, and he didn't know that, because I'd fled without saying a thing. His torment would last a long time. They surely had the police on their side; they would take him to a police station. Was he sitting in a dark cell at this moment? I'd cast him into the abyss of my revolt and forgotten him. I'd thrown him to the crocodiles of my tribe. They would stop at nothing, because it was a matter of honour, and they were insane.

The old night watchman continued his soliloquy, and through the mists of the moment, I began to see clearly how things would unfold. My desertion had brought me up against a dune as tall as a century. I would never find Marvoud. My mother, faced with all her people, would never reveal her secret. They would trample over all the Rayhanas of heaven and earth to get back their damned *rezzam*. They would give up all their possessions, even their lives, to restore it to its place in front of the chief's tent, so the old men could stroke their beards and gaze at it, indulge it so it would carry on delivering nice lies for them to tell. Neither Mbarka nor Hama could do anything for me now; of course they would rush to my aid if I asked them to, but they had no power; they would only get caught up in a storm of ill winds.

Abdou's mother would be cursing me; I'd brought misfortune to her home after she'd offered me shelter, opened her arms to me. I'd repaid her by involving her son in a venture that had nothing to do with him, and now he was rotting in prison. The real jailers would not be the police, but my uncle and Mahjoub, the 'tribe's benefactor'.

The watchman had placed a tea pot, glasses and a small gas brazier on the ground. He continued to speak. 'The world is finished, my child. It's finished. You know Emir Abderrahmane? You know the *hella*? No, you don't. I'm not angry with you, child, all young people today know nothing. No, I'm not angry, but Emir Abderrahmane was something. You should've seen him, in his time. He was a real leader, and his *hella*, his court, was the ultimate court. It had noble warriors, it had marabouts guided by God, griots who really knew how to tell stories and sing, blacksmiths who could chisel beautiful works and could speak well too, and of course slaves, and Emir Abderrahmane was at the centre of it all. He was in charge, never mind the authorities, the governors, the colonels. He was the leader. You know, once there was an election here and we all voted 'yes', as the Emir wanted us to, and when they counted they only found three 'no' votes. Three 'no' votes and two thousand 'yes' votes, I think. The governor of the district said, 'That's good, you voted well!' but the Emir said, 'No, it's not good. Three imbeciles voted against me. We must find them.' So they looked and they did find them. It was an old woman, Souelma, who was blind, an idiot slave, and the third was one of the Emir's own chauffeurs. Naturally he was dismissed! Ah, Emir Abderrahmane was something. I'm telling you this because yesterday some people came here and said to everyone, 'There will be elections soon, and you should choose freely.' The Emir used to say, 'This is how you should vote.' He was a real leader, and he was a great poet too… You know, everything belonged to him, his own possessions and everyone else's too, but he didn't take advantage. He was something, the Emir. When he passed by he used to greet me, he even spoke to me a little, even gave dates and sweets to my oldest daughter, who's married now. Does the governor speak to people? Never! All of that's over. The Emir is dead and my animals are too. There's nothing now. That's why I'm a night watchman.'

The sky was beginning to dress in its purple clothes for dawn, the stars beginning to blink, saying goodbye to the world. Was this the same sky that hung over the camp? There, the herdsmen would already be milking the animals, people would be waking up to pray, children would be stuttering their first words of the day. There, life was already shaking itself awake, dreams had been packed away, things were returning to their places. Here in the city, people waited for the sun before making their beds and going to work. There, they had stolen my child, here they were hunting me down... I had nowhere to hide. Abdou would be sent to prison, they had money and the authorities on their side, they would bribe and buy to find me and the sacred drum. Abdou knew nothing, though they would torment him for a long time. They would go after Hama, then Mbarka. They would bring the sky tumbling down to find the totem that was nestled there, powerless, inside the suitcase I was sitting on.

The old watchman handed me a glass of tea. I thanked him in a small voice. I felt the hot, bitter liquid run down my throat and into my stomach. I nearly retched.

'So, you're a relative of Halima's,' he said. 'She'll be here soon, to light the hammam fires. You must tell her to pay me. The others have paid, because, you know, all the shops here give me a little money at the end of the month, for watching them. Halima is late. I know she has her problems, but I do too. I have a family to feed.'

I realised this man was alone. He was speaking because no one ever listened to him, because no one listened to the voices of others here. Everyone was deaf because they didn't want to hear about anyone else. I gave him back the glass.

Suddenly the man began to sing. His voice was tuneful and strong. He gestured with his hands and smiled broadly at me. His large eyes danced in the tentative light. I could distinguish his features now. He seemed to have got younger. I knew the words of the song he was singing. They described the celestial beauty of Fatimetou, the daughter of the prophet, her arms, her legs, her face, her back. The description conformed to our conventions for describing beauty, and made her sound like one of the girls from our camp. I realised the old watchman was singing about me. He'd understood my distress and wanted to encourage me. This was his way of saying, 'You're beautiful, and your future is ahead of you.' I didn't know how to react, because I could see no future.

Halima had arrived. Her mouth gaped when she saw me.

'Rayhana? What are you doing here at this time? Why have you got a suitcase?'

I didn't know what to say. Should I tell her everything? It was hard for me to stand, my legs and my head felt so heavy, and I still felt like vomiting.

'I need shelter. Just for a little while.'

'But why? You're staying with Hama's sister.'

'My family and the police are looking for me.'

'What?'

'First they took my child, then they took away the only arms holding me up, they arrested Abdou, Hama's nephew.

They want to send me to prison.'

'That's enough! Don't say any more, I don't want to know. I want to be completely in the dark. I don't want trouble. Hama is my friend, but that's not a good enough reason. Please, sort it out yourself. I want nothing to do with it.'

I was almost relieved by her response. I'd expected it. I felt as if the race was over. There was no more track to run down, there were no more dunes to scale, there were no new horizons to dream of. To push on ahead would be to hurt other people, to bite the hands that had fed me. I had no words, there was no point.

The old watchman, who'd heard the conversation, was trying to pick up my suitcase.

'You'll come to my house,' he said. 'It's not near, and it's not pretty, but you can rest there while you're waiting.'

I thanked him, took up my burden and walked away from him.

I saw nothing. The anonymous crowd was gone, the cars were gone, the road had dissolved, the whole city had died. It had drowned in its own vanity, in the lies of its inhabitants; the sand had reclaimed what belonged to it. The domes of the law courts still reached proudly towards the sky, but they were obscured by the thick smoke that came from the belly of the earth. The tribal drum and the books of law crackled in the flames I'd lit. The smoke curled up into the air, to denounce the treason and the lies, so the whole world could see and hear. I raised my arms and screamed, 'They took away my love, my little soul, but look at their idols burning! They're nothing, they only help them to do wrong and steal!' My cries found no echo: no other sound broke the silence. My stomach and breasts were bruised from the bites of this brownish morning that had swallowed everything, but I was moving forward again, roaring so that the shimmering courts and the sleeping town could hear me, 'Abdou, who you've taken from his family, is innocent! It's me who stole your idol, it's me who's burning and insulting the law!' No one answered. I was alone, the world had evaporated around me. In the distance, I suddenly saw a movement, the smallest glimmer, something beckoning to me, perhaps. I ran with all the strength I had left in me. I saw Marvoud, lying asleep, naked, on a bed of rubbish. I leaned over to pick him up, but all that was there was a red stain. It spread outwards until I was looking into a well of fire, a pit of molten lava hidden beneath the detritus of the city, a spinning hell-hole that contained the whole suffering universe. I felt an overwhelming fatigue. All I wanted was to close my eyes and never open them again, to be gone from the world and all of its people. I picked myself up, dumb and destroyed.